SHOWDOWN

AT THE

SALOON

One bullet hit the bar and the other two smashed the pier glass on the wall behind the mahogany. Torn scarcely flinched. Moving with deliberate calm, he dropped the empty shotgun on the bar and drew the Colt Peacemaker. He heard Booth's Lightning dry-fire, and at the same time saw Preacher setting up for a shot from behind the cover of the overturned deal table. The Peacemaker boomed three times. Torn sent all three bullets into the table closely grouped. The slugs pierced the table and slammed into Preacher. The gunslinger fell backward; his trigger finger spasmed and two bullets clanged against the green tin of the saloon ceiling. Preacher's boot heels drummed briefly on the floor, and then his body went limp in death.

Also by Hank Edwards

THE JUDGE

WAR CLOUDS

GUN GLORY

TEXAS FEUD

STEEL JUSTICE

LAWLESS LAND

BAD BLOOD

RIVER RAID

BORDER WAR

Published by
HARPERPAPERBACKS

THE JUDGE

DEATH
WARRANT

Hank Edwards

HarperPaperbacks
A Division of HarperCollinsPublishers

This is a work of fiction. The characters, incidents, and dialogues are products of the author's imagination and are not to be construed as real. Any resemblance to actual events or persons, living or dead, is entirely coincidental.

HarperPaperbacks *A Division of* HarperCollins*Publishers*
10 East 53rd Street, New York, N.Y. 10022

Cover illustration by Tony Gabriele

First printing: August 1993

Printed in the United States of America

HarperPaperbacks and colophon are trademarks of HarperCollins*Publishers*

10 9 8 7 6 5 4 3 2 1

CHAPTER 1

HE CAME DOWN OUT OF THE PINE-COVERED RIDGES BE-tween the White and Niobrara rivers, a tall lean man dressed in black, riding a lanky claybank horse. When he saw the Sand Hills country of Nebraska stretched out to the horizon in front of him, he knew at a glance it was arguably the best cattle land a man could find between Abilene and the Absarokas.

Others before him had reached the same conclusion. Prior to the War Between the States, and in the years immediately following that conflict, most of the beef had come from Texas. Railroads had forged across the prairie, starting with the Union Pacific, and the cattle had come north from the Lone Star State to railheads in a succession of wild and woolly trail towns. And then a cattleman had been struck by a bright notion—why wear yourself down to a thin frazzle driving thousands of ornery longhorns up trails fraught with just about every kind of peril imaginable, when north of the placid Platte were twenty thousand square miles of peerless range called the Sand Hills?

Most of these tough-as-saddle-leather ranchers didn't know geology from a hole in the ground. They didn't know how the Sand Hills had turned out so custom-made. Especially since, in their opinion, most of the rest of Nebraska wasn't fit for raising jackrabbits. Let the grangers squabble over the rest of Nebraska, they said; let the plow pushers break their backs scarring up the land with their middle busters. The cattle kings had their hats set for the Sand Hills. Raising cows a hundred miles from the railheads made a lot more sense than doing the same thing a thousand miles away in Texas!

As Clay Torn crossed the grasslands, he saw plenty of grazing cattle on the open range. The land had been molded into gentle valleys, softly rounded hills, long ridges, conical peaks—all covered with a rich mantle of grass. Not much shade, though. Trees were as scarce as hen's teeth. Summer was nearly spent, and for that Torn was grateful; it was plenty hot enough to suit him.

His destination was the town of Valentine, and in the three days it took him to cross the grasslands to reach the vicinity of the Cherry County seat he saw an abundance of wildlife. It was the water that made this country a paradise for bird and beast. There were hundreds of lakes and ponds and wet meadows, teeming with ducks, geese, and cranes. For dinner one day he hooked a fat and sassy trout out of a stream which ran clear and sweet as good white wine, and the next day he bagged a plump ring-necked pheasant in the scrub-choked breaks of the Niobrara. The deer were as thick as fleas, mule and white-tailed both, and antelope, too, as well as grouse and prairie chicken and wild turkey. Only the beaver and the bison were in short supply; it was 1877, and the trappers had done for the former what hidehunters were well on the way to doing for the latter.

For the first two days in the Sand Hills Torn did not see another living soul. He knew there had to be range riders out here, but it was an awfully big country, and the ranches were immense. The cattle barons didn't know how to think small. Towns were few and far between, roads were rarities. He had heard there were gangs of rustlers who hid out in the breaks, and occasionally renegade Pawnees stirred up trouble. But such hazards did not much concern Clay Torn.

He didn't mind the solitude. He was by nature something of a loner. It hadn't always been so. In his youth, growing up the eldest son of one of South Carolina's most influential planters, he had been an outgoing young gentleman endowed with all the social graces, and fond of the company of others. Especially that of his beautiful fiancée, Melony Hancock. Life had looked bright indeed, back then, with a secure future of wealth and prestige—a life of thoroughbred horses, fine food and bonded whiskey, custom-made broadcloth suits and English fowling pieces.

Then the war had come. Torn had left family and fiancée behind to ride off to give his all for the glorious cause of Southern independence. He had quickly learned that there was nothing glorious about war. But he served with distinction as one of the Confederacy's most dashing and daring cavalry officers. At Gettysburg—East Cavalry Field—he had watched his younger brother Stewart die in his arms and had been captured by the Yankees. Sixteen months of incarceration in the prisoner-of-war camp at Point Lookout, Maryland, had followed his capture. Sixteen months of sheer hell, thanks in large part to a sadistic federal sergeant named Karl Schmidt.

Schmidt had grown up in the slums of Shytown, the son of wretchedly poor German immigrants. Before the war he had worked as a railroad bull, and for a time earned a living as a pugilist. Both jobs had provided him with the license to do what he most liked to do—inflict pain on others. Clay Torn had epitomized everything Schmidt envied and, as a result, despised: money, breeding, intelligence. He had made breaking Torn's spirit his mission in life.

And while Torn won this battle of wills, the suffering Schmidt had put him through had irrevocably changed him. To survive brutality he had become brutal. Killing Schmidt, escaping from Point Lookout, and making his way back to South Carolina in the chaotic last days of the dying Confederacy, he had found his family dead, his home, Ravenoak, burned to the ground by Sherman's invaders, and Melony Hancock vanished. Rumor had it Yankee deserters had abducted her and fled west.

Westward Torn had gone—twelve long years ago— searching for Melony. He did not know if she was still alive; if she was a thousand miles away or over the next hill. He carried her memory with him, and something inside him refused to let go of it. In his possibles were a handful of love letters she had written him during the war. Each one had been read countless times around lonely campfires. In the pocket of his somber black frock coat, near his heart, was a daguerreotype—Melony, prim and pretty, sitting before a gaudy backdrop in a Charleston portrait studio just weeks before Torn had gone off to war. He had shown the photograph to hundreds, probably thousands, of strangers. Had they seen her? Most said no. A few said maybe. But all the leads had been false. Still, he kept looking. It was his obsession. Sometimes he thought it was the only thing that kept him going.

These days he was a federal circuit judge. The job suited him. It gave him license to wander far and wide in his relentless search for the woman he had loved and lost, and an excuse to dispense with men who lived outside the law, and who by their cruelty and callous disregard for others reminded him of Karl Schmidt. Ghosts from the past haunted Torn—Melony and Schmidt—and the life he led seemed foreordained. Certainly it was influenced by those ghosts he tried every day to lay to rest.

Since leaving home to serve the Cause, his life had been a long road with very little on the wayside but trial and travail, and the dozen years he had spent west of the Mississippi had educated him on the subject of the frontier's violent nature. He was not one to let down his guard, or to take anything for granted. Lean and quick, he knew how to use his fists, as well as the .45 Colt Peacemaker on his hip, and the Winchester 44/40 repeating rifle in the saddle boot.

But the weapon folks associated with Judge Torn was the blade secured in a custom-made shoulder rig concealed beneath his dusty black frock coat. It had once been a Chicopee saber, Schmidt's property—the weapon Torn had used to slay his tormentor. Not long after his escape from Point Lookout, the saber had broken, and Torn had honed the blade to its present fifteen inches of razor-sharp steel. It was an unique weapon, an integral part of the legend already grown around this hard-bitten, soft-spoken man in black with eyes gray like gunmetal and an Old Testament concept of right and wrong.

Though he had gone days without seeing another human being, and seemed to have this whole big, wide-open country all to himself, he was not the kind of man to be caught unawares by sudden violence. So, on the third day out, not too far by his calculations from Valentine, when the gunshot ripped the heavy heat, startlingly close, he was not alarmed. The claybank jerked its head and fiddle-footed, snorting. Torn steadied the cayuse with low-pitched horse talk and listened for more gunshots.

They came, fast and furious, and Torn got a fix on the location, less than a quarter-mile east. He gadded the claybank in that direction without second thought.

He came to broken country, where a tributary of the Niobrara had cut deep creases in the hills. Checking his horse on a scrub-covered spur, he spotted several men crouched in a rock outcropping below and to his left. They all wore yellow dusters, with bandannas masking their features, and they were firing down into a dry wash where a man cowered behind the carcass of a just-killed horse. Every now and then this man would return fire with his side gun, but to no effect—he did not even lift his head to sight a target.

On the frontier, a man minded his own business and did not buy into another's trouble. That was accepted practice, and no one who followed such a wise course needed to fear censure from others for doing so.

But the odds here were four to one, and Torn's well-defined if simple sense of fair play was offended. The bandannas made his choice easier. This was no righteous posse cornering a lone long rider. The four in the rocks were obviously bushwhackers on dark desperado business.

So Torn did not hesitate. Dismounting, he tethered the claybank, drew the Winchester long gun from its scabbard, and moved on down the spur with the stealth of an Apache, intent on dealing himself into the fray.

CHAPTER 2

ETCHED IN THE UNYIELDING STONE OF TORN'S SOUL WERE A handful of hard and fast rules by which he lived. They were rules to which he adhered because they kept him, a man prone to violence in a violent land, on the right side of things.

One of those rules was never to kill a man unless that man was trying to kill him first.

Torn had a clear shot at three of the four masked men in the rocks. They had their backs to him, and no inkling of his presence. But there was another rule, and it had to do with back shooting. He opted for the next best thing. His first shot winged one of the dry gulchers, the bullet smashing the man's shoulder, slamming him forward. The ambusher fell, his blood a bright red smear on the stone, to grovel in the pale dust.

Jacking another round into the Winchester's breech, Torn fired again. The bushwhackers were quick to react to this new threat, and Torn's second bullet shimmied harmlessly off rock. The three masked men started slinging lead in Torn's direction. Torn threw himself flat as bullets clipped the scrub concealing him. He crawled downslope, knowing they were aiming at his smoke, and when he rose up on one knee and sent two more rounds into the rocks he was twenty feet from his previous position.

The bushwhackers had good cover, so Torn's bullets damaged nothing but stone. The man he had wounded was crawling, trying to get into some cover. Torn could have killed him, but refrained. The injured dry gulcher was out of the fight, and that was good enough.

Again the bushwhackers saw his smoke, again they altered their aim. Again Torn moved. Gun thunder rolled across the hills. Though outnumbered three to one, Torn held the high ground, and the dry gulchers were now pinned in a cross fire. The man hunkered down behind the dead horse was still blasting away. Torn sensed he was no hand with a gun, but even the worst shots sometimes got lucky, and the bushwhackers knew that. The outcome was never in doubt. Torn's arrival had turned the tables and there wasn't anything the three masked men could do about it.

After a minute or two of making smoke, they broke and ran. One gave his wounded partner a hand while the other two laid down a heavy covering fire to keep Torn busy. Bullets buzzed through the brush like a swarm of angry hornets. Torn ate dirt. Several slugs came too close for comfort.

They were bad hombres on bad business, and they

were doing their damnedest to ventilate Torn, so his first rule no longer applied. It rubbed against Torn's grain to just belly-down in the brush while they made good their escape. Steeling himself for the impact of a bullet—a sensation with which he was familiar—he jumped up and started running down the slope of the spur, weaving through the scrub. The bushwhackers were darting into a draw at the foot of the spur. Torn figured they had secreted their horses there, and he thought he might be able to cut them off.

Reaching the rim of the draw, he found two of the dry gulchers already mounted. A third was assisting the wounded man into his saddle before turning to his own horse, held by one of the mounted men.

At first they did not see Torn hurtling downslope toward them. Torn tossed the Winchester from right hand to left and drew the Colt Peacemaker. When the Colt spoke, the bushwhackers answered. They had no luck hitting their target. Torn was moving fast, running headlong, and they were sitting on horses which pranced and pivoted under short rein, agitated by the flat booms of the hog legs going off next to their heads.

Torn had no better luck, at first. His targets were obscured by a choking cloud of dust and gunsmoke. One of the dry gulchers shouted, turned his horse, and savagely dug spur. His horse jumped into a gallop. The others followed. Torn altered the angle of his descent. The Peacemaker's hammer fell on an empty chamber. Cursing, Torn shoved the Colt into its holster, stopped, and raised the Winchester's stock to shoulder. The bushwhackers were fast pulling away. He knew he would have time for one shot, maybe two at the outside, before they were out of the draw and out of sight.

His first shot grazed the thigh of one of the masked men and struck the horse beneath him in the withers. The animal's front legs buckled and it fell, hurling the rider forward. The horse got up, trying to bite the pain of the bullet wound, as animals will. The man lay still.

The other riders kept going, and Torn moved down into the draw, loping at first, then slowing to a walk as he got closer to the fallen ambusher. The man lay facedown. Was he unconscious, or dead? Or playing possum? Torn worked the Winchester's action. He fired from the hip. The bullet kicked up dust a foot from the man's head. The bushwhacker didn't move. Torn relaxed a notch and stepped closer.

The two uninjured bushwhackers came out of nowhere, guns blazing, their horses stretched out at full gallop.

Torn whirled, prepared to stand his ground in a hail of hot lead and shoot it out. He had been under fire too many times to lose his nerve.

The Winchester jammed.

He couldn't believe it. The 44/40 had never let him down before. It was a habit to keep his weapons in perfect working order.

But this was neither the time nor the place to puzzle over the repeater's failure.

A hasty glance revealed the holster on the fallen man's hip was empty. Torn turned for the man's horse, circling nearby, still trying to bite at its wound. Two strides and Torn was leaping into the saddle before the cayuse knew what was happening. The animal balked and crow-hopped, in no mood to be ridden, but Torn had spent a lifetime around horses, from the thoroughbreds for which Ravenoak had been justly famous to the frontier mustang. He won the horse over with a firm hand, reining it sharply and kicking it into a canter, bent low in the saddle. The injured horse broke into an awkward gait.

There was a carbine in the saddle boot, one of the old Spencers which had come into use the last year of the war. It sported a tubular magazine capable of holding seven cartridges, but when Torn worked the action he discovered that the gun was empty.

A cold chill started at the base of his spine and worked its way up. One weapon jammed, two empty. Bad luck at the wrong time: two key ingredients for getting killed. In the heat of battle he had made a mistake—failing to pause long enough to reload the Colt Peacemaker. In a minute he would know if it had been a fatal mistake.

"I'm snakebit," he muttered, trying to kick a little more speed out of the horse. Getting the reins in his teeth, he drew the Peacemaker, got the cylinder open, and began to thumb shells out of his belt and into the chambers.

He figured the two bushwhackers would chase him down and finish him off, and resolved to turn on them once he got the Colt fully loaded. Charging straight at the enemy in the saddle, guns blazing—the frontier equivalent of jousting knights—suited him much better than running.

But the dry gulchers checked their horses near where their colleague had fallen. One handed his reins to the other, who kept shooting at Torn, then jumped down, picked up the fallen man and tossed him across the saddle like he was a sack of grain. Vaulting back aboard the overloaded horse, straddling the cantle, and retrieving his reins, the bushwhacker turned his horse and lit a shuck. His partner sent two more rounds in Torn's direction, turned and dusted out.

Torn checked his horse, considered pursuit, discarded the idea. His mount was carrying a bullet and wasn't going to go very far very fast. The wound wasn't fatal, but it had its effect on the animal's performance. Holding the horse to a walk, he returned to the place where the dry gulcher had been thrown. Now that he had the leisure to do so, he searched for and found the man's side gun. Curious, he stepped down to retrieve the weapon. It was a bone-handled Remington Navy. There were six notches carved into the yellowed bone.

A gunslinger.

It was the only clue Torn had to the identity of the four masked men. They had gone to extremes to avoid leaving evidence behind. Two had put their lives at risk to rescue their wounded associate, and they had done so without knowing whether he was alive or not —they hadn't stopped to check. Live body or corpse, they had retrieved it.

Torn checked the horse for saddlebags. There were none. He looked for a brand, but it had been burned off with a running iron. He uncinched the three-quarter rig and pulled it to the ground. Then he took the curb bit out of the animal's mouth, unstrapped the bridle and let the horse go. Bending down, he checked the rig for mark of ownership. A lot of men carved their names or initials on their tack. Nothing. He untied and unrolled the blankets, found a spare shirt in the hot roll, and that was all.

Retrieving his Winchester, and securing the Remington under his gun belt, he walked on out of the draw and into the dry wash. He passed the rock outcropping, headed for the carcass of the horse, unable to tell if the lone rider who had been the intended victim of the four bushwhackers was still cringing behind the dead animal.

"Hold it right there!"

Torn froze. The voice, pitched high with nervous tension, came from behind him.

Quite calm, Torn said, "They're gone. I hit two of them. Might have done one in, I'm not sure."

There was no response. Torn started to turn around.

"Don't move!"

Torn held his hands away from his sides, dropped the empty Winchester. It wasn't any good to him at the moment anyway.

"Easy," said Torn. "Keep in mind I was the one who saved your bacon."

"Who are you?"

"Clay Torn. Federal judge."

Another nerve-racking pause. Then, "Turn around."

Torn obeyed.

The man emerging timidly from the rocks looked as out of place as horns on a jackrabbit.

He had "city slicker" written all over him, from the top of his derby hat to the soles of his hand-tooled shoes. Dust and sweat could not entirely mask the quality of his tailored broadcloth suit. A knee was ripped out of one trouser leg, and a seam had split in the shoulder of the coat. His silk cravat had come out of his shirt collar and now lay askew on one shoulder, and there was a bullet hole in the crown of his derby. The gun in his white-knuckled grasp was a silver-plated .38 Forehand & Adams. Spectacles pinched the bridge of his nose.

He was a young man, redheaded, a little on the frail side, and terribly sunburned. His complexion was pale, and his tender skin was obviously unaccustomed to the harsh elements of the big sky country. He was highly agitated, his knees wobbly, his hands trembling.

"Calm down," advised Torn. "That gun's got a hair trigger. What's your handle, son?"

"Handle? Oh, you mean my name. My name is Terrill. Andrew Terrill. Most people call me Andy."

Torn's steel-cast eyes narrowed. "Any kin to Lane Terrill?"

Strong emotion twisted Andy's features.

"He's my father."

"Then we'd better have a talk," said Torn grimly. "Because your father is part of the reason I've come all this way."

CHAPTER 3

ANDY TERRILL LOWERED THE .38 REVOLVER.

"You said you are a federal judge?"

Torn nodded. "Seems there's a dispute between your father and some homesteaders. Or maybe you'd prefer to call them squatters."

Terrill adamantly shook his head. "Just because I have his blood in my veins doesn't mean my father and I see eye to eye. But the problem is not as simple as you make it out to be."

"The grangers want the dispute settled peacefully, in a court of law."

"Your court."

"Looks like. As far as I know, there hasn't been any killing. Plenty of shooting, though, from what I've been told. Your father's range riders have been terrorizing the settlers, or so they claim. Burning their

16

crops, shooting up their homes, killing their mules and milk cows."

"Sounds like you've already passed judgment."

"Not really. I don't know enough of the facts."

"My father came to the Sand Hills ten years ago. The land was for the taking. He and another cattleman named Quarles agreed that the Rosebud River would be the boundary line between their spreads. The river changed its course last spring. My father claims the old course should still be considered the boundary. If it isn't, he loses over a hundred square miles of range. Rather than risk a range war with my father, Quarles let the homesteaders move into the disputed area. To act as a kind of buffer."

"You don't talk or dress like the son of a Nebraska cattle baron," remarked Torn.

"It is a long and sordid tale of woe," replied Andy. "My mother was a schoolteacher from Boston. Why they ever got married in the first place is a mystery to me. You would be hard-pressed to find two people with less in common. My father is rough and profane. Never stepped foot in a schoolhouse. Once said he had no use for any book except the Bible. Drinks hard, fights hard. Doesn't give anybody any slack. My mother was a delicate, God-fearing woman. She liked good books and nice things."

"Was?"

"She died two years ago," said Andy, grief twitching the corners of his eyes and mouth. "She couldn't endure my father for very long. When he moved his outfit up here to the Sand Hills she left him and took me back to Boston with her. I was ten years old at the time. Her family took us in. Her brother and uncle are both wealthy gentlemen. One's a banker, the other's in shipping. They saw to it I received the best education money could buy."

"So you and your father were never close."

Terrill's smile was bitter. "When I was younger I despised him for what he did to my mother. She loved him but couldn't live with him—had to leave him, finally, even though it broke her heart to do so. I've been called a mama's boy. But I've been corresponding with my father for several years now. Haven't been back here, though. I never expected to come back. But I studied law, and I suppose Father thought he might need some legal advice."

"They've got lawyers in Nebraska," said Torn. "Some good ones. Why send for you, especially since the two of you disagree on so many things?"

"Maybe because my legal advice is free," surmised Terrill. "But no, actually, I think my father wants his son back. Oh, he's too proud to come right out and say so, but I think this is just an excuse. If you're wondering where I stand, I, too, know only what I've heard, or rather what I've read in Father's letters. But I oppose the use of force for any reason, least of all fighting over land. My father has plenty of range, more than he could ever use. A hundred square miles is just a tiny fraction of the T Bar Ranch. But he doesn't like to lose. Especially to plow pushers, as he calls them."

"Those four men who dry gulched you—I don't know who they are, but I guarantee they're not farmers."

"I have no idea," confessed Andy, adjusting his seebetters and scanning the breaks all around with scared eyes. "I took the stage as far as Cody, and then all the drivers walked off the job—wage dispute, I gather. It's a small-time stage line, Judge, and I wouldn't be surprised if it goes bankrupt before long. So I wired ahead to Valentine, to get word to the ranch, left my baggage with a freight outfit, and rented a saddle horse. They were waiting on the road. I tried to run. This is as far as I got. I suppose they must have been road agents. Highwaymen, as they used to be called. I've always thought 'highwayman' was a much more romantic name, don't you?"

"Nothing romantic about being bushwhacked," said Torn. "You sure can talk up a storm."

Andy blushed. "Especially when I'm afraid. But words are a lawyer's stock in trade, aren't they? Talk, and talk some more, until you get the point across." He flashed an infectious, boyish grin. "Someone told me that if you don't have a case you just keep talking, until the judge or jury awards you the decision just to shut you up."

"I hope you don't expect that to happen this time."

"No. You strike me as a fair-minded man. And I'll never be able to repay you for saving my life."

"I don't think they were highwaymen."

"Why not? What else could they have been?"

"I don't know."

"Will they come back?"

Torn shrugged, nodded in the direction of the dead horse. "Gather all your possibles and let's get going. Valentine's not too far east of us, and we're burning daylight."

"But . . . am I to walk?"

"I've got a horse up yonder. You can ride him. I'll walk."

"I couldn't . . ."

"Might be ten, twenty miles," said Torn, brusque. "I can walk that easy. I'm pretty sure you can't."

Andy's feelings were hurt. "No. I suppose I couldn't. I'm not as tough as you are, Judge Torn. I grew up on the frontier, but I must confess I never cared for the life. I inherited my mother's love for literature and luxury. I am a barely adequate horseman and an atrocious shot. People must learn to accept their limitations, don't you agree? It's pointless trying to be someone that you're not, and I . . . Judge? . . ."

But Torn was walking away, shaking his head ruefully, and making for the spur where the claybank was waiting.

CHAPTER

4

THEY FOUND THE ROAD TO VALENTINE AND STUCK TO IT.
Torn kept an eagle eye on their back trail, but the day
ran its course without a hint of pursuit. With the twi-
light came the threat of rain. While the Sand Hill hol-
lows filled with the indigo blue of coming night, and
the crests blushed with the fiery orange and rose
hues of sunset, an ominous bank of storm clouds
rolled in from the southeast, stabbing at the earth with
jagged yellow pitchforks of lightning. Thunder, muted
by distance, rolled across the land.

"It's coming a real frog-strangler," said Torn.

"Won't we make Valentine today?" asked Andy, eye-
ing the fast-moving line of black-bellied clouds with
apprehension.

"Doesn't look like it," replied Torn, wondering if
Andy Terrill was so far dandified that he was scared of

thunder and lightning. "But we'll push on as long as we can."

Ten minutes later they spotted a pair of riders coming west down the road toward them. Torn tensed, expecting more trouble. A panic sound escaped Andy's throat. The youngster cast about in search of some place to hide. But there wasn't any, and Torn had no intention of hiding, anyway. There were only two, and if they were hostile, two-to-one were the best odds he'd had yet today. He didn't figure Andy Terrill into the equation. The boy—for though he was twenty, Torn thought of him as a boy—was a liability rather than an asset.

"Are you any better with a rifle?" snapped Torn, without much hope.

"What?" gasped Andy.

"Are you better with a rifle than you are with a pistol?"

Andy was striving to collect his wits. "I, um, well, to be honest, Judge, I . . ."

Exasperated, Torn tossed him the Winchester. While walking he had cleared the repeater's action of sand, and now the rifle was loaded and in working order once more. Andy fumbled the catch, almost dropping the Winchester.

"Get down off that horse," said Torn. "You make too good a target in the saddle. If shooting starts, hit the ground and shoot back. Try to hit something. Anything, long as it isn't me."

Andy dismounted, and Torn took charge of the reins. Grasping the leathers in his left hand, he rested his right on the Colt Peacemaker in his holster.

The two riders wore range clothes, but they weren't wearing masks. Both were young, lean, and leathery.

Cowboys from hat to heel. One was a black man. Torn could tell they had teethed on branding irons. As they checked their ponies twenty feet away, one of the lathered horses turned sideways, prancing, and Torn spotted the T Bar brand on its hip. He relaxed a little. At least these hombres were wearing their bandannas around their necks where they belonged, and riding horses that hadn't had identifying marks burned off their hide.

The cowboys looked back and forth between Torn and Andy and then at each other, as though each expected the other to do the talking.

It was the black cowboy who spoke first.

"Howdy."

Torn nodded.

"Looks like rain."

"Looks like," agreed Torn.

The other cowboy squirmed in his sweat-stained saddle, lips thinned with impatience. He combed a thick black mustache with thumb and forefinger, muddy-brown eyes flicking to the hand Torn had resting on the Peacemaker.

"Expectin' trouble, I see," he drawled.

"Expect the worst," said Torn, "and hope for the best."

The black cowboy said, "Name's Jericho Gentry. This here's Dusty Burcham. We ride for the T Bar."

"Thank God," breathed Andy fervently. In the failing light he had not seen, and had not thought to look for, the brands on the horses.

The cowboys looked at him.

"I'm Andy Terrill," said Andy.

Now they were staring.

"You work for my father," explained Andy.

Jericho and Dusty decided to stare at each other for a while. Gentry was the first to recover.

"You're Lane's boy?"

"Yes," said Andy, suddenly grim. He realized now why they had been staring so hard.

Distant thunder drumrolled across the Sand Hills.

"Well," drawled Dusty, looking at Andy as though Andy were some kind of strange critter he'd never seen the likes of before. "Cut me off at the knees and call me shorty." He tore his gaze away from Andy's fancy duds and glanced at Torn. "Who are you?"

"Clay Torn."

But Torn was not sufficiently interesting to steal Dusty Burcham's interest away from Andy for long. Those muddy-brown eyes swung back to Andy almost immediately. They reflected fascination as well as dismay.

"Jericho." He sighed. "Reckon our string's played out for good?"

"Don't know, Dusty."

"I reckon it is. I reckon we might as well say adios and make tracks."

"Don't know. Maybe we owe Lane more than that."

"What are two talking about?" asked Torn.

"The T Bar," said Dusty. "I've worked for Lane Terrill for almost eight years. Jericho for longer. First job I ever had. Couldn't ask for better. Wandered out this way from Alabama and Lane hired me on. The T Bar's been my home. But everything ends, don't it?"

Not much enlightened, Torn said, "You came out looking for him." He nodded at Andy. It was a statement, not a query.

Jericho nodded. "Rode all day."

"So what is all this talk of quitting?" asked Andy. "If you like your job, why give it up?"

Jericho drew a long breath and looked off yonder, squinty-eyed. For the first time Torn comprehended the grief in both men. They were cowboys, and therefore tough in mind and soul as well as body, and the last people one would expect to see wearing their feelings on their sleeves.

"The T Bar's the only home I've ever had," said Gentry. "Just like Dusty here. My roots are here. But Lane Terrill is dead, and so maybe the T Bar is, too."

"Dead!" gasped Andy. "My . . . my father's . . ."

"Shotgun. Full choke. Close range," said Dusty, angrily biting off the words. "Goddamn sodbuster did it."

Stricken, Andy turned his back on them and walked off down the road. Torn watched him until he stopped, twenty paces later, then turned back to the T Bar range riders.

"When did this happen?"

"Yesterday."

"Who killed him?"

"Sonuvabitch's name was Caldwell."

"Was?"

Dusty's smile was chill as winter ice. "He got his neck stretched. Hemp justice."

"Judge Lynch," said Torn.

"Don't care for the word 'lynch', mister," said Dusty, who looked like the type who was ready to fight at the drop of a hat—or a word he didn't approve of.

"And I don't like the idea," said Torn.

"Am I s'pose to care what you like?"

"Did you lynch Caldwell?"

Dusty fired a glance at Jericho. "No. We didn't get the chance."

"Don't put me in," said Gentry. "I wouldn't have no part of it, no how, Dusty. I seen my own pa lynched, back in Alabama." He looked at Torn, his chin lifted a defiant inch. "My pa hit a man in the face, an overseer who was layin' my ma's back open with a cat-o'-nine-tails." Back at Dusty, he said, "I don't hold with that kind of business."

"Neither do I," said Torn.

"Just who the hell are you?" asked Dusty, thoroughly provoked.

"A federal judge."

Dusty let his breath out through clenched teeth, all at once, like he had been punched in the breadbasket.

"I'll want to know who hanged Caldwell," warned Torn.

Dusty glowered. His eyes were harder than flint.

"T Bar riders, I reckon," added Torn.

"You might be biting off more than you can chew, Judge," said Dusty.

"Stop it!"

Startled, they all turned as Andy Terrill came striding back up the road. Torn felt the ground vibrate as thunder rumbled across the darkening land again.

"I know what you were saying earlier," Andy told Dusty Burcham. "You took one look at me and decided the T Bar was finished. That since I have inherited the ranch you don't want to work for the T Bar anymore. You don't think I can handle the job. Well, maybe you're right. Maybe I can't fill my father's boots."

"You can sell out to Quarles," said Dusty. "He wants the T Bar so bad he can taste it."

"Maybe I will. Or maybe I'll try my hand at running the ranch."

"You?" Dusty was incredulous.

Andy turned to Torn. "Let's get moving. I would like to be present at my father's funeral."

"So would I," said Jericho. "We knew you was coming, so they held off until tomorrow for the buryin'. I'll go back with you, Mister Terrill. How 'bout it, Dusty? You ain't never been a quitter."

Burcham grimaced. "Maybe I owe Lane that much," he allowed, but he didn't sound too sure.

"Maybe you owe him more," said Jericho. "Maybe I do, too. I reckon he'd want us to stick by his boy, don't you?"

"Storm's comin'," grumbled Dusty. He swung his horse sharply to head back in the direction of Valentine.

"How far to Valentine?" Torn asked Jericho.

"Won't make it 'fore nightfall. With this storm, we'll see it come morning. There's a place about five miles down the road. Swing station run by Old Man Taylor. Seein' as how the stage ain't running, he'll loan out a horse, like as not."

Torn nodded, swung aboard the claybank, and helped Andy Terrill up behind him.

They rode on.

CHAPTER

5

It RAINED MOST OF THE NIGHT AND THE NEXT DAY WAS downright dismal. Thunder rolled and lightning ripped and the clouds sometimes seemed to touch the ground. The rain was a never-ending misery, at times just a drizzle, at other times a downpour drenching the Sand Hills in silver sheets.

The streets of Valentine became treacherous quagmires of mud and muck. Not even the dogs ventured out into them, preferring instead to cower beneath the boardwalks and raw clapboard buildings. But for warm yellow lamplight in a few windows, the town looked deserted.

Valentine's cemetery lay on the east edge of town. Here, scores of headstones and weathered wooden crosses marked final resting places. But Lane Terrill had made it clear he had no desire to rest in peace in the local bone orchard. As a result, his funeral took place a half mile south of Valentine, across the Niobrara River, on a long grassy slope where a single lodgepole pine stood, stark and grand in its isolation.

This was T Bar range, and the tree was called Two Mile Pine, for a reason no one seemed now to recall. There was a ferry across the Niobrara, but the river was running high, wide, and handsome, and some of the townfolk who in better weather might have attended the burying stayed home.

Torn, Andy, and the two T Bar riders paused at the crest of the slope, a hundred yards above the grave site, and sat their horses a moment.

"Looks like we made it in time," said Jericho.

Torn estimated there were twenty-five mourners clustered under a canvas tarpaulin stretched out between poles over the grave. He saw a plain white casket on the soggy ground beside the six-foot hole. A dozen saddle horses and several buggies stood downslope at a picket line. Farther north, obscured by the rain, curled the silver serpent of the Niobrara, and beyond it, Valentine.

"Come on," said Andy, strangling on emotion.

Dusty's voice was hoarse. "Reckon we'll stay up here. It's close enough."

Torn understood. Dusty and Jericho had worked for Lane Terrill a long time, and had counted it a privilege to do so, and they were hurting. But they didn't need to shed tears into Lane's grave to prove it. As he followed Andy down the slope, he noted with approval that the two cowboys removed their hats.

Heads turned in the congregation as Torn and Andy approached. Torn figured the word was out that Lane's son was coming, and folks were curious. But they couldn't tell much about young Terrill. Having left his baggage in Cody for later freighting to Valentine, Andy had headed for the T Bar with only the clothes on his back. The generous old gentleman at the swing station where they had nighted, and who had given them an extra horse, had also provided Andy with a slicker and a flop-brimmed Kossuth hat to replace his shot-to-hell derby. Andy had removed his spectacles due to the rain. As a result, he did not look out of the ordinary, for which Torn was grateful.

There were a few women in the crowd, and as a matter of course Torn peered closely at each one. It was habit now, hoping against hope that someday he might look up and see Melony Hancock. People could change a lot in fifteen years, but he knew he would recognize her immediately. Of course, none of the women present at the funeral of Lane Terrill fit the bill, and Torn felt that familiar cutting emptiness he never could seem to come to terms with, regardless of how often he experienced it.

A pair of rain-soaked, mud-smeared grave diggers stood slightly apart from the others, leaning wearily on their shovels, beyond the shelter of the tarpaulin. A preacher was positioned at the head of the grave, a Bible open in his hands, and as he concluded the service he glanced up at Andy and Torn, who remained on their horses.

" 'O God, whose mercies cannot be numbered, accept our prayers on behalf of the soul of Thy servant departed, and grant him entrance into the land of light and joy, in the fellowship of Thy saints, through Jesus Christ, our Lord, Amen.' "

"Amen," chorused the mourners.

The preacher nodded to the grave diggers, who

lifted the casket by means of underslung ropes, and with what reverence they could muster and tired muscles would permit, lowered it into the grave.

Torn glanced at Andy. The young man's shoulders were bunched, his head lowered, and he was gripping the pommel of his saddle with both hands, as though he wanted to twist the horn clean off the rig.

"I know," said Torn. "I lost my whole family. Alone and empty—that's how you feel, and it hurts like hell, and you figure it's gonna hurt like that the rest of your days. But in time the pain will ease up, at least enough so you can handle it."

Andy nodded. He wanted to thank Torn, but didn't trust his voice. It helped to know that others had endured what he was now suffering, and survived.

The service over, the mourners began drifting away, down to their horses and buggies, a few slogging through the mud of the road ox-bowing down the slope toward the ferry. Most threw inquisitive looks at Torn and Andy, but only two approached. The first was the preacher. The second hung back to let the man-of-God have his say.

"I'm the Reverend Dunaway." There was a sour expression on his long, sallow face, but his tone was amicable, and Torn surmised that Dunaway was one of those men who wore a perpetual scowl, whether unhappy or not. "Were you gentlemen acquainted with the deceased?"

Torn waited for Andy to respond. Terrill hesitated, and Dunaway misinterpreted.

"Forgive me for prying," said the preacher. He had been on the frontier long enough to know that there were some men you didn't get too nosy about. He held his Bible beneath his slicker, protecting it from the rain. "It's simply that I know all the others. Local people. Many of them in my flock."

"Where's the headstone?" asked Andy.

"Uncut, as yet. You see, we've heard that Lane's son is due to arrive shortly." Dunaway cocked his head. "Would you by any chance be . . ."

Andy nodded.

"Your father never stepped inside the church. When once I asked him why, he explained to me that he felt closer to the Almighty astride his horse, riding the open range. I suppose a person can commune with God in different ways and in different settings. We are, in the end, judged by our good works, not our church attendance."

"You think my father went to heaven, Reverend?"

The question surprised Dunaway. Torn detected a bitter bite to Andy's words.

"Why, yes, I hope so," said Dunaway, but he didn't sound all that convinced.

"What about the man who killed him? Caldwell? What about his soul, Reverend?"

"I pray for it. But murder is . . ."

"Unforgiveable? What if Caldwell believed it was the only way to protect his home and family? Might that not be construed as self-defense?"

Torn thought Andy sounded like a lawyer giving his final summation before the jury.

"There is no excuse for taking the life of another. Not even self-defense. I cannot believe you would defend the man who killed your own father."

"But what if I forgive him, Reverend?"

Dunaway was perturbed. He sensed that Andy had gotten the better of him in a debate on a subject Dunaway felt he owned.

For his part, Torn was intrigued. Here was a side of Andy Terrill he hadn't seen before. He wasn't sure if it counted as a good side or a bad side, but at least it showed the young man could be assertive, and had spirit. He wasn't much of a shot, but when it came to talk, he could use words the way a sharpshooter used bullets.

Dunaway took his leave, and the second man stepped in to take his place. He was a tall, lantern-jawed fellow, with shoulders ax-handle wide and legs horse-warped. Middle-aged, with iron gray hair and mustache, but Torn could tell he had the strength and vitality of a much younger man. His eyes were black and hard, like polished obsidian.

"I couldn't help overhearing," he said. "You are Andy Terrill. I want to present my sincerest regrets. My name is . . ."

"Joshua Quarles," said Andy. "I remember you. I'm surprised to find you here."

"Why? Because your father and I had a few differences? Nonsense. We came to these hills together, son. Staked out our claims, lived as neighbors for ten years. I admired the hell out of Lane Terrill. He was quite a man. It takes quite a man to carve a cattle empire out of this land and hold onto it."

"The same compliment applies to you, then," remarked Torn.

Quarles squinted suspiciously at Torn, wondering how Torn had meant the comment.

Andy, smiling bleakly, said, "And you're wondering if I'm man enough to handle it, aren't you, Mister Quarles?"

"You've got Lane's blood in you. I reckon you might. But do you want to? That's the question."

"And if I don't?"

"I'm not one to beat around the bush," said Quarles, flashing a meaningless smile. "I'll buy the T Bar from you."

"But what if I don't want to sell to you?"

"You don't like me much. I'm sorry about that. But what have I ever done to you, Andy? Nothing, really. Your father and I did butt heads, but you have to expect that of the two biggest ranchers in Cherry County. Still, I respected him. And, I'll be honest, I'm the only man around with enough money to pay what the T Bar is worth."

"A man who has to tell you he's being honest usually isn't," said Torn.

Quarles's black gaze swung back to Torn and locked on.

"Who are you?"

Torn told him.

"You and I will have to talk, Judge. Later. Andy, I hope you will keep my offer in mind."

"I won't forget it."

Quarles turned away, striding to the last horse left on the picket line. Andy dismounted and walked closer to the grave. The grave diggers stopped filling the hole, but at Andy's nod they proceeded to shovel mud. Torn remained mounted. He could hear the mud slap against the pine casket, now six feet down, and he watched Quarles riding along the serpentine road toward the Niobrara ferry.

He had a hunch there might be more burying in Cherry County before long.

CHAPTER

6

WHILE JERICHO AND DUSTY ESCORTED ANDY TO THE T BAR
Ranch, Torn rode into Valentine, looking for the sheriff.

The road from the Niobrara ferry became the
town's main street, and one of the first businesses he
passed was Kostmyer's Livery and Wagon yard. He
figured the claybank had earned a double dose of oats
and a good brushing down, so he turned in. Kostmyer
turned out to be a gaunt, gruff old-timer in overalls.
He was solemn as a funeral. Torn paid a day in ad-
vance and asked the whereabouts of the jail house.

"On down the street. Other side," said Kostmyer
tersely.

Torn nodded thanks and headed out, with his small
black valise and the scabbarded Winchester. The valise contained a change of clothes, a couple of statute

books, a straight razor, mirror and bar of lye soap, ammunition for his side gun and repeater, and the cherished handful of letters written many years ago. This was the sum total of Clay Torn's worldly possessions.

"But if you seek the sheriff," called Kostmyer, "you'll fare better checking the Bull's-eye Saloon."

Torn turned, eyebrows raised in silent query. He detected a trace of sarcasm in Kostmyer's voice.

"Ben Mackey gets his lunch out of a bottle," said Kostmyer, with asperity. "And since he's in Treadway's pocket, so to speak, it's only logical that you'd find him in the Bull's-eye."

"Treadway?"

"Olin Treadway. Owns the Bull's-eye. And the dance hall across the street called the Silver Eagle. And he just bought Cooper out. Cooper owned another saloon. Now Treadway owns just about everything on Keno Street. That's our local tenderloin district." Kostmyer looked sternly disapproving.

A burly blacksmith was working at the forge just inside the livery's big double doors. He wasn't paying Torn or Kostmyer any attention as he labored relentlessly on a horseshoe. In a routine as natural to him as breathing, he would tong the shoe into the orange-glowing coals, then hammer at it on the anvil, then douse it in the nearby barrel of water while pumping the forge bellows to keep the fire crucible-hot.

"They say the cowboys from all the ranches hereabouts need such a street," continued Kostmyer, "where they can sow their wild oats. And Treadway runs it. Except for that woman's place. That Rose Pendergast."

"What?" Torn couldn't believe his ears. "Rose Pendergast?"

Kostmyer nodded. "Runs a brothel called the Yellow Rose."

"I'll be damned," breathed Torn.

"May well be," said Kostmyer, sanctimonious, "if you are the type to frequent such an unGodly place."

"Rose Pendergast is an old acquaintance," said Torn.

"She is a fallen woman," declared Kostmyer, "and you should . . ."

Torn turned his back on the man and stepped out into the drizzling rain. He headed north up Main, pursued by the clanging cadence of the smitty's hammer against the stubborn iron.

Keeping as much as possible to the boardwalks, he slogged through the muck at the mouths of the alleys between the clapboard buildings. The street was a rusty-red quagmire.

Before finding the jail, he came across the Plainsman Hotel. The doors to the lobby were open, so he used the boot scraper to remove a few pounds of Nebraska from his feet and crossed the threshold, stepping around a barefoot boy who sat in the doorway. The boy wore faded overalls. His straw-colored hair was tousled, his face smudged with dirt. He absently scratched a redbone hound curled up beside him. The hound growled at Torn without bothering to lift its grizzled head. The boy's shy smile was apologetic.

The desk clerk was engrossed in a dime novel, and didn't notice Torn until Torn laid his Winchester on top of the counter.

"Need a room?" asked the clerk, disposing of the

wildcat literature beneath the counter, as though ashamed of being caught with it.

"That's why I'm here."

The clerk produced a leather-bound ledger, pen, and inkwell. "For how long, sir?"

"As long as it takes," replied Torn, signing in.

"Torn?" The clerk's eyes widened. "Clay Torn? The judge?"

"Right."

The clerk was beside himself. "Judge Torn! It's . . . It's a real honor to have you staying in the Plainsman, sir!"

"Why is that?"

"Why? Why?" The clerk wrung his hands. "Because, sir, you're famous. Why, you're probably the most famous man ever stayed under this roof. You have quite a reputation, sir. Oh yes. Your name strikes fear in the heart of every owl hoot on the frontier. They say you've killed a hundred outlaws. Undertakers buy your drinks wherever you go. They call you Judge Colt, because you pass sentence with a .45 Peacemaker. Is it true you killed Big Blue Ketchum and five of his gang in a Dodge City gunfight?"

"You read too many books." Torn sighed. "Room?"

"Number Four, Judge. Overlooks the street. I'll show you. Here, let me carry . . ."

Torn confiscated the key. "I carry my own."

As he headed up the narrow stairs, he noticed that the barefoot boy and his redbone hound had vanished from the doorway. He gave it half an hour before everyone in Valentine knew he was in town.

Depositing rifle and valise in his room, Torn returned to the street and found the jail house. The cells were empty, as was the sheriff's office. He negotiated a muddy alley and emerged on what he assumed was Keno Street—a handful of saloons, a dance hall, barbershop, and cowboy emporium.

Also, fifty yards south of where he stood, a two-story clapboard house, painted yellow, vaguely Victorian in design, with green shades on the windows. From the lintel of the veranda depended a sign with a yellow rose painted on it.

Torn's steel-cast eyes narrowed behind the veil of rain dripping from his hatbrim.

"A small world," he muttered.

Bittersweet memories pulled at him from the yellow house, drawing him like a hot flame drew a moth, and he actually took a step in that direction, but stopped himself. He had business to tend to. Old friends, like Rose Pendergast, could wait.

So he bent his steps in the other direction, and came to the Bull's-eye Saloon.

He pushed through creaky bat wings and paused to survey the long room with its green tin ceiling, dirty fly-specked walls, sawdust-covered floor. The mahogany bar stretched along the right wall, backed by pier glass and bottle-laden shelves. To his left were a dozen deal tables. In the back was the hash counter, presided over by an Oriental in a white apron stained with blood. The place reeked of charred beef, stale sweat, cheap aged-in-the gullet red-eye, and old tobacco smoke. Torn had seen a hundred saloons just like it.

Not counting the Oriental, there were five men in the saloon.

One worked behind the bar, a scrofulous old-timer with a scraggly beard, a patch over one eye and an ornery expression on his deeply seamed face. He had the look of a man who had tried everything in life and found absolutely none of it to his liking. He glanced at Torn like he wished Torn would turn around and get the hell back out in the rain where he belonged.

Two others were playing a desultory game of Mexican Sweat at one of the deal tables. One glance was all Torn required to know them for what they were. Gun hawks. Not cowboys from local spreads, that was certain. Torn recalled having seen no horses tied to the hitching posts outside. Which meant these gallop-and-gunshot boys resided in Valentine.

The fourth man, over at the hash counter, was cut from similar cloth. He was a giant of a man, too busy working on the steak the Oriental cook had just brought him to bother looking around at Torn.

The fifth man was belly-up to the bar, elbows hooked on the mahogany, one foot hiked up on the brass boot rail—a paunchy man gone to seed, with a tin star pinned to his vest. Like the barkeep, the badge-toter shot a quick look at Torn. Disinterested, he returned his attention to the empty shot glass in his hand. As though wondering where the whiskey it had recently contained had gone to, he turned it morosely in his hand, this way and that, and then tapped the bar with it, plaintively summoning the bartender.

"Another dose of Old Overholt, Patch."

As the apron produced a bottle, Torn crossed to the bar. The two men at the deal table watched him like a pair of turkey buzzards. Moving slow, Torn reached under his coat and brought out the Remington Navy with the bone grips, the gun he had retrieved from the site of yesterday's gunplay. He dropped the charcoal-burner on the bar as the sheriff was raising the full-to-the-brim shot glass to his lips.

"Christ!" yelped the badge-toter, sloshing the liquid bravemaker as the six-shooter clattered on the mahogany. With a sulky glower, he sucked whiskey off his hand.

"Sheriff Mackey, I presume," said Torn.

"Yeah. Who are you?"

"I was told I might find you here."

"I asked you once," said Mackey, bellicose. "Who the hell are you?"

"Clay Torn. Federal judge."

A chair leg scraped against the floor. Torn's flinty gaze flicked to the pier glass. He could see the reflection of the two men at the deal table. They were still seated, but one had moved his chair slightly, and now both had only one hand visible on top of the table.

"You know those two, Sheriff?" asked Torn.

Mackey looked over his shoulder, like he hadn't been aware until this moment that he was sharing the saloon with other patrons.

"Yeah. I know them."

"Friends of yours?"

"I wouldn't say friends. What business is that of yours?"

"Maybe you could ask them if one of them lost this thumb-buster."

Mackey looked at the Remington, noticed the notches.

"That's a hired gun's hog leg."

"I know," said Torn. "And you're sitting in a nest of bad men, Sheriff. Tell you what. Your jail's empty. I'll help you haul them over there, and we'll check the wanted posters. I have a hunch those boys are papered. What do you think?"

"Tell you what I think," said one of the men at the table. "I think you're fixing to cross over the River Jordan, friend."

CHAPTER 7

"WHAT ARE YOU TRYING TO DO?" MACKEY ASKED TORN IN A panic-stricken voice that screeched like a rusty gate hinge. He stepped away from Torn as he threw an anxious glance at the men sitting at the table. But Torn's hand lashed out and gathered up the front of Mackey's shirt. He yanked the sheriff back to the spot where he had been standing before.

"Introduce us," said Torn, his voice calm, a faintly mocking smile touching his lips.

"You're loco," rasped Mackey. "You know who they are?"

"I know what they are. They're the same breed tried to dry gulch Andy Terrill yesterday. Might even have been a couple of these boys. There were four in all. All wearing slickers, and bandannas covering their faces.

43

I shot two of them. Had any shot-up dry gulchers ride into Valentine lately, Sheriff?"

"I don't know what you're talking about," whined Mackey. He was scared right down to the ground.

Torn despised cowards who tried to pass themselves off as brave men.

"How did a yellow-belly like you ever get that tin star, Mackey?"

"Let me go," whimpered Mackey, sagging a little at the knees, because both gun hawks at the table were standing now.

"I'll do the introducing," said one of the hired guns. "I'm Booth. This here's Preacher."

Booth was a slight man who stood crooked, one shoulder hitched higher than the other, one leg hipshot. He wore concho-studded pants and a buckskin hunting shirt that in places was black with grime. His side gun was a Colt Lightning, and he sported a sheathed Arkansas Toothpick as well.

Preacher—the man who had made reference to the River Jordan—was a long, lanky, gimlet-eyed hombre with a thick black mustache. He slowly draped his black duster behind a matched pair of Dance revolvers in the tied-down, cross-draw holsters on his narrow shanks.

"I don't feel like going to jail today," sneered Booth. "How about you, Grizzly?"

The name suited the man at the hash counter—a big, hirsute bear of a man. He wasn't interested in the proceedings, at least not enough to stop working on the two-inch-thick steak the Oriental cook had burned for him. He merely grunted over a mouthful.

"Who do you work for?" asked Torn. "Quarles?"

Booth grinned. His grin was crooked, too. "You're shooting in the dark, Judge."

"He's a damn federal judge," growled Patch, the bartender, like he was completely fed up with the whole situation. "You can't just gun him down, you idjits."

"The hell we can't." Booth laughed. "Just stand back, old codger, and watch us."

"I'm telling you," snapped Patch. "Not here. Treadway would kill you, Booth, kill you deader'n last Sunday's sage hen, if you made that kind of trouble for him in his place."

So they work for Treadway, thought Torn. But why would a saloon owner need a gang of gun hawks on his payroll? There was more to this business—much more—than met the eye.

"Treadway can kiss my boots," hissed Booth. "Ain't no way this big-talking sonuvabitch is gonna put me in some iron cage."

Sheriff Mackey sensed that lead slinging was imminent, and he was directly in the line of fire. With a strangled cry he tried to tear loose of Torn's grip, but it was a grip like an iron vise. In desperation, Mackey groped for the six-gun on his hip.

Torn punched him in the face. Mackey slumped, blood spewing from nose and mouth. Torn hurled him at Booth as Booth drew the Colt Lightning. The sheriff shattered the table and went down in a shower of splinters and playing cards. Booth and Preacher jumped out of the way, buying Torn a few precious seconds.

Out of an eye-corner, Torn saw Patch reaching under the mahogany. Torn didn't wait to find out what he was reaching for. Snatching up Mackey's bottle of Old

Overholt, he broke it over the barkeep's skull. Patch collapsed, out cold, and Torn vaulted over the bar and dropped behind it as Preacher's Dance revolvers and Booth's Colt began to thunder.

Bullets splintered the mahogany. Staying low, Torn spotted the sawed-off shotgun Patch had been after, on a shelf next to a supply of reasonably clean shot glasses. Apparently the barkeep had not been all that opposed to violence in the Bull's-eye as he had made out to be.

Grabbing the greener, Torn crawled on down the bar a ways before breaking the shotgun open to check the loads. Booth and Preacher were still peppering the bar with hot lead, the latter hollering "Praise the Lord!" and "Hallelujah!" like a just-saved sinner at revival. Taking a deep breath, Torn got his legs under him and rose, swinging the greener around and firing one barrel of double-ought.

Both Booth and Preacher had rattler-quick reflexes. It was a requirement in their profession. One dived left, the other right, and the double-ought pockmarked the wall behind them. They were looking out for themselves, each hoping it would be the other that Torn went after with the second barrel.

Torn took a split-second to scan the room before pulling the greener's second trigger. Sheriff Mackey was crawling on his belly for the door, making funny sounds and leaving smears of blood from his ruined mouth and broken nose on the floor. In back, the Oriental cook was departing hastily through a rear door, chattering shrilly in his native tongue.

Oddly enough, the man named Grizzly was still at the hash counter consuming his dinner, ignoring the mayhem. Torn had never seen anything quite like it, and he had seen some cool customers in the war. Grizzly was obviously a man to be reckoned with if he was so inured to sudden violence that he could keep his head, not to mention his appetite, while bullets were flying. But since he apparently wasn't going to buy into the fracas right away, Torn decided it was safe to deal with Booth and Preacher first.

Booth was up and running in a crouch, heading for the end of the bar. Preacher had dived behind a deal table and overturned it to provide more cover for himself. Torn fired the second barrel at Booth. The double-ought caught the gun slick in hip and leg and knocked him sprawling. Cursing at the top of his lungs, the wounded gunslinger fired a few rounds at Torn. One bullet hit the bar and the other two smashed the pier glass on the wall behind the mahogany. Torn scarcely flinched.

Moving with deliberate calm, Torn dropped the empty shotgun on the bar and drew the Colt Peacemaker. He heard Booth's Lightning dry-fire, and at the same time saw Preacher setting up for a shot from behind the cover of the overturned deal table. The Peacemaker boomed three times. Torn sent all three bullets into the table closely grouped. The slugs pierced the table and slammed into Preacher. The gunslinger fell backward; his trigger finger spasmed and two bullets clanged against the green tin of the saloon ceiling. Preacher's boot heels drummed briefly on the floor, and then his body went limp in death.

Torn shot a quick glance across the gunsmoke-shrouded room at Grizzly. The big man had stopped eating. Now he was looking at Preacher's corpse, his expression unreadable.

Thunder rolled angrily across the sky, rattling a

loose pane of glass in the saloon's front window. Torn walked to the end of the bar. Mackey was crawling under the bat wings out onto the rain-slick planks of the boardwalk. Booth was writhing in agony on the floor, trying to reload the Colt Lightning, but his fingers were slippery with his own blood, and he kept dropping bullets. Torn kicked the pistol out of his grasp. Booth cursed some more, his crooked face a snarling rictus of hate. He groped for the Arkansas Toothpick at his side. Torn cocked the Peacemaker and aimed it right between the gun hawk's eyes.

"Want to join your friend on the other side of that river?"

Booth glowered. If looks could kill, Torn would have dropped dead then and there. The gun slick hurled his blade away.

"A jail cell beats a pine box," said Torn, and turned toward the rear of the saloon. "You. Grizzly. If you're heeled, get rid of the hardware."

"I ain't done nothing," grumbled the big man surly.

"You ride with these two?"

Grizzly nodded.

"Then it's guilt by association, I reckon. Drop it or draw it."

Grizzly thought it over. Didn't sound to him like Torn much cared which way he decided to go. The Walker Colt he tugged out from under his belt was a big pistol, but it looked mighty small in his ham-size hand. He dropped it, and the sixteen-pound relic clattered on the floor.

"Now get over here and carry your friend to the jail house."

Grizzly lumbered over. Torn felt the floor move with each step the goliath took. Close up, the man loomed over him. Torn wasn't sure but that Grizzly wasn't actually bigger than his namesake. His arms and legs were big around as tree trunks. Torn backed up a step to stay out of reach. Grizzly grinned. It wasn't a pretty sight. Even his teeth were big, like crooked yellow tombstones, with pieces of steak stuck between them.

Grizzly misconstrued Torn's cautious backstep for fear. "Don't get too close," he growled. "If I get my hands on you I could snap your spine like a dry twig. I could tear your head off at the shoulders. I could break your arms right off. Wouldn't bother me none. I like to do it. I done it before."

"You like to hurt people, Grizzly?"

Grizzly grinned. "Yeah, I like it. I like it 'specially when I squeeze their skulls and watch their eyes pop out."

Torn wondered how many bullets a man like Grizzly could take before going down. He had three beans left in the Peacemaker's cylinder, and that didn't make him feel very secure.

"I'd hate to have to kill you, Grizzly," he said, and grinned right back. "They'd have to bury you in a wagon bed."

"There'll be another day," said Grizzly, supremely confident. He bent down and picked up Booth without the slightest strain. Slinging the wounded gun slick over his shoulder, he trudged through the bat wings.

God, I hope not, prayed Torn, following in the giant's wake.

CHAPTER

8

Upon arrival at the jail, Torn locked Grizzly in one cell and the gunshot Booth in the other. Somewhere between the Bull's-eye Saloon and the jail house they had picked up the barefoot boy and his redbone hound, both muddy and soaking wet. Torn sent him to fetch the local sawbones. The boy took off at a sprint, the baying hound loping along behind him. While they waited for the doctor, Torn plucked the badge from Sheriff Mackey's shirt.

"Hey!" exclaimed Mackey through a mouthful of blood.

"This badge is too much for you to handle."

"You can't do that!" protested Mackey, thick-tongued, and edging toward belligerence. "I was elected, dammit. Oh God you bwoke my nose! You got no right to . . ." A fresh wave of pain distracted him, and he sank into a chair behind a scarred kneehole desk and moaned wretchedly, covering his face with his hands.

The doctor arrived, black bag in hand. He took a look at Booth, bleeding in his cell, and then at Mackey, bleeding at his desk, and said, "Good Lord." He sounded disgusted.

"The one in the cell needs you worse," said Torn.

"I can see that," snapped the sawbones crossly.

"I'll have to check that bag first."

"You most certainly will not."

Torn held out a hand. "Give me the bag. I'm in no mood for any more righteous indignation."

The doctor heard something in Torn's voice, or saw something in Torn's eyes, that made him believe that last statement. He relinquished the bag. Torn opened it, searched the contents, returned it.

"What were you expecting to find, may I ask?" asked the piqued physician.

"A gun."

"I heal people, mister. I don't go around shooting them. I don't like guns. I don't own one."

"Fine," said Torn. "I'll have to lock you in the cell with him."

"Do what you have to do."

Torn did. Then he turned his attention on the erstwhile sheriff.

"Who lynched the farmer, Caldwell?"

The question caught Mackey off guard.

"Dunno. Wasn't there."

"Did Caldwell shoot Lane Terrill?"

Mackey spat blood on the floor and nodded miserably.

"How do you know? Were there any witnesses?"

"Folks knew Caldwell had threatened Lane's life," spoke up the doctor from Booth's cell. He was cutting away the gunslinger's blood-soaked pants leg, and didn't bother looking up. "He was heard to say that if any T Bar riders came on his homestead again he'd put holes in Lane. And Lane was found dead not a half mile from Caldwell's place."

"Who found him?"

"Lane's horse found its way back to the T Bar. The cowboys found blood on the saddle. They backtracked the horse to the body. Lane had been shot in the back. Ten gauge. Both barrels."

"But who found the body. I want names."

"I don't have any," said the doctor. "I'm just telling you what I've heard. Just T Bar riders. That's all anybody in town knows. Why don't you go ask them? But they stick together."

"I will," said Torn. "Back to my original question. Who lynched Caldwell?"

"We assume they were T Bar men. His wife said hooded men came riding in that night. Dragged Caldwell out and strung him up. She didn't see their faces. They wore their bandannas on their noses."

"Caldwell might not have been Lane's murderer," said Torn.

"Who else?" mumbled Mackey.

"Caldwell's not the only homesteader Lane Terrill was riding roughshod over. And who else around here was crossways with Terrill?"

"What are you getting at?" asked the doctor. "You mean Mister Quarles, by any chance?"

"You're a fool if you mess with Quarles," said Mackey, wiping a scarlet drool from the corner of his mouth. He was a mess; his face was swelling and dis-coloring.

"Christ!" muttered the sawbones.

Torn walked over to Booth's cell. The doctor had finished cutting away the pants leg, and was counting buckshot. White as a sheet and drenched in a cold sweat, Booth was groaning and swearing through clenched teeth.

The sawbones shot a withering look at Torn. "You do this?"

"He was moving fast and I was rushing my shot," said Torn, laconic. "Otherwise, I would have called in the undertaker and not bothered you."

"You're the federal judge rode in today, aren't you? A man like you—representing law and order."

Torn had to wonder why the doctor was so dead set on giving him a hard time. Whatever the reason, it was beginning to get under his skin.

"Save the chin music for later, Doc, and patch up my prisoner."

The doctor stood and came to the bars. "You don't remember me, do you?"

Torn took a real good look. Valentine's sawbones was an elderly gentleman. His broadcloth coat and trousers were rumpled, like he'd slept in them for a month of Sundays. His iron-gray hair needed a brush. He looked a bit seedy, but there was integrity in his craggy face, and his gaze, aside from being hostile, was steady and honest.

"Guess not," said Torn, unable to jog his memory.

"We weren't formally introduced. Name's Jonah Wingate. My shingle was hanging in Lincoln a couple years ago. I was there when that bunch of rowdies led by that old hide hunter, Rankin, came in, ran the sheriff off, and took over. And I was there a few weeks later when you came along. Up until then there hadn't been any killing. Rankin's boys played hell with the good folks of Lincoln, but no bloodshed—not until you showed up. That's when the killing started. All of Rankin's gang, and two townsmen besides. Decent folks. Innocent bystanders. Shot dead."

Torn nodded bleakly. "I remember. By Rankin's men."

"Is that what you tell yourself so you can sleep at night?"

Torn was angry, but he did not voice his anger; he did not feel as though he held the moral high ground.

"I've always thought you pushed Rankin too hard," continued Wingate relentlessly. "Backed him into a corner. Didn't give him any slack. In my opinion you provoked that fight. You pressed too hard. You . . ."

"All right," rasped Torn.

Softer, Wingate said, "My guess is you did the same thing today."

"Just like you said, Doc," concurred Mackey with enthusiasm. "Went right in and stirred up trouble. Said he was gonna haul these boys to jail, and them not havin' done nothing. Just sitting there minding their own business."

"You mean Treadway's business," said Torn dryly. "What does Treadway need with men like these, Doc?"

"That's none of my affair. This country breeds men like this. And like you, Judge. You may think you're better than they are, because you stand on the right side of the law, but I'm not sure there's two bits worth of difference between the lot of you."

"Maybe not," allowed Torn.

"When I heard you were coming to settle things, I knew Valentine was in for it. It'll be just like Lincoln all over again, won't it, Judge? You settle things with a gun instead of a gavel."

"Hey!" barked Booth, perturbed. "Dig this buckshot out of me, Wingate."

Wingate turned his frosty gaze on the gunslinger. "You want chloroform?"

"Hell no," said Booth. "But I'll take a bottle of red-eye."

"Check the desk, bottom drawer," Wingate advised Torn.

"Wait a minute!" yelped Mackey, as Torn removed a bottle of whiskey from the desk. "That's mine."

"You gutless wonder," growled Booth. "Treadway gives you all the free whiskey you can drink and you begrudge me one lousy swig out of your lousy bottle of who-hit-john."

"Nothing in here belongs to you anymore," Torn informed Mackey.

"Go wait in my office, Ben," Wingate told the ex-sheriff.

Mackey headed for the door, sulking. He paused at the threshold.

"You'll rue the day, Torn."

He hastened out, uninclined to tarry for fear of Torn's reaction to this idle threat.

Torn handed the bottle to Wingate through the cell's strap iron. The doctor passed it on to Booth. While Wingate dug through the paraphernalia in his black bag, the gun hawk took a long drink. He glowered at Torn.

"Gonna hang around and watch, Judge? Well, that's fine by me. You count that double-ought as the doc here digs it out of my hide, 'cause I'm gonna put a bullet in you for every pellet comes out of me, and that's a promise."

Wingate glanced over his shoulder at Torn, with a wry smile on his lips.

"Doesn't sound like you have too many friends in Valentine, Judge."

Torn didn't reply. His thoughts drifted to the big house on Keno Street, the one with the sign of the yellow rose above its door.

CHAPTER 9

AS THE DAY CAME TO AN END, SO DID THE RAIN.

Once Doc Wingate had finished ministering to Booth and taken his leave, Torn pocketed the cell-door keys and ambled back over to Keno Street.

For a while he stood in the dusk shadows across the street from the Yellow Rose. Lamplight blazed behind the green shades on the windows. Four horses were hitched out front. Eventually Torn got up the gumption to cross over and climb the veranda steps. Summoned by his tug on the brass bellpull, a petite Oriental girl answered the door. She was a slender, raven-haired beauty in a red silk *cheongsam*. Putting her hands together, she bowed him into the down-stairs hall.

"Hat please," she said.

Torn handed over his headgear. "I've come to see Rose Pendergast."

"Gun please."

"She's an old friend."

"Gun please."

Torn unbuckled his gun belt, gave it to her. He did not volunteer the saber knife in its shoulder rig beneath his frock coat, or the Remington Navy under his belt at the small of his back.

"Tell her its Clay Torn come to call."

"Follow me please."

He did so, through double doors into a parlor.

"Wait please." She bowed herself out.

A window was open, and a breath of damp air stirred the green shade, slipping past it to play with the crystal teardrops of a milk-glass lamp on a taboret of inlaid wood. The furniture was upholstered in velveteen. The Persian carpets were plush underfoot. The pine floors were polished to a rich red sheen. The walls were covered with damask.

Across the hall came the sound of a piano, the laughter of a man and a woman. Not Rose—Torn knew that immediately. There was another parlor, behind another set of double doors, where business was being conducted.

Torn was standing next to a Wurlitzer piano, determining that the tranquil landscape in a gilded frame on the wall above the instrument had been rendered by a talented pilgrim named Gainsborough, when Rose entered the room.

She wore a black silk wrapper adorned with a gaudy red and gold dragon. Her long and lustrous hair was the color of a Kansas wheat field drenched in sun. Her complexion was honey and cream, and her red lips were heart shaped. Torn remembered what a pleasure they were to kiss. She was, he thought, as beautiful as ever. Only the eyes had changed. They were still that exquisitely deep indigo blue. But, even filled as now with joy, they reflected a jaded and weary soul.

"Hello, Clay," she said, in that husky voice that never failed to stir his blood.

"Hello, Rose. The years have been kind. You're lovelier than when I last saw you."

She laughed. Hers was a vibrant, spontaneous laugh, as lusty as the lady to whom it belonged.

"Still a Southern cavalier at heart, aren't you? I've been expecting you. Heard you were coming to Valentine."

"Never expected to find you here. It's a small world."

"Speaking of finding someone . . . have you . . . ?" Second thoughts gave her pause.

Torn's smile was strained around the edges. "No. No I haven't."

"I'm sorry. I shouldn't have mentioned it."

"No matter."

"But you're still looking."

Torn looked away. Her gaze was too intense. He knew the truth would hurt her.

"Yes."

"I guess you'll never give up. Just like Sir Gawain and the Holy Grail."

"You're a hopeless romantic, Rose."

"Look who's talking! Want a drink? Bourbon, isn't it?"

He nodded, secretly pleased that she remembered. She moved to a sideboard covered with decanters.

As she poured, he said, "You've done well for yourself. Not hurting for business."

"There's a good reason why it's the oldest profession in the world, Clay."

"Why did you quit the trail towns?"

She shrugged and brought him his drink. "The wild side of trail towns have short lives. I got tired of moving from railhead to railhead. Sedalia to Wichita to Dodge to Ogallala. There are plenty of cowpokes in the Sand Hills, Clay, and its not seasonal."

"Settling down?"

She handed him his glass. Her fingers brushed his. She pulled her hand away as though his touch had shocked her. Her smile was pensive as she turned away. Moving to the taboret, silk swishing seductively, she took a cheroot from a humidor of hammered silver. Struck a China match to life on the lid. Drew the smoke in deep and let it out in pale blue streams through her nostrils, unconscious mimicry of the ferocious dragon on her wrapper. Brows arched, she cut those indigo eyes at him. Torn recalled she always looked defiant when she smoked, as though daring others to make some comment. But Torn didn't mind. He had told her before—he didn't care what a person did as long as he, or she, didn't do it in the street and scare the horses.

"I heard about the gunfight at the Bull's-eye Saloon," she said, deftly changing the subject. "You tangled with Treadway's hired guns."

"Well, there's one question finally answered."

"I gather Treadway wasn't there."

"You sound scared when you speak his name, Rose. I never knew you to be scared of anything."

"I'm not." Then she equivocated. "Well, maybe a

little. The man is . . . dangerous. Not dangerous like you. He's . . . he's mean and brutal and . . . unprincipled. Listen to me." She laughed at herself. "Me, talking about principles."

"I think you have principles. I trust you."

She seemed surprised. "You do?" she asked girlishly.

"Sure. So what's going on around here, Rose? No one else is willing to talk. I know you'll tell me the truth."

"It's cold and hard. Have you met Joshua Quarles?"

"At Lane Terrill's funeral."

She smirked at that. "Quarles has nerve. I'll give him that much. You see, Quarles and Treadway are thick as thieves. Quarles wants to own all the range in Cherry County. The T Bar stands in his way. Treadway wants to own Valentine—at least this part of Valentine. Keno Street. And I stand in *his* way."

"He needs hired guns to protect himself from you, Rose?" Torn smiled.

Rose wasn't amused. "He wants to own me, too, by the way."

Torn's smile faded. He understood.

"How does it all fit together?" he asked.

"What do you mean?"

"Treadway's hired guns. The grangers. The murder of Lane Terrill."

"A river changed its course. Simple as that. Josh Quarles knew Lane wouldn't let all that graze go without a fight. And he didn't fancy a range war with the T Bar. So he moved the homesteaders in. They're caught in the middle. He gave them the land for next to nothing. What's a hundred square miles to a man who's playing for much bigger stakes—all of Cherry

County? Sounds like a mighty fine gesture, doesn't it? But Quarles is a cold-blooded bastard. He's using those poor dirt farmers. He was hoping Lane would do just what he did—start trouble. He was counting on something happening to Lane, just the way it happened."

"So you believe Caldwell killed Lane."

"I wasn't there. I can't say. What are you going to do, Clay? You came here to settle the dispute over ownership of that land. If you say the river changing its course was an act of God, you'll be doing all those plow pushers and their families a big favor. If you go the other way, and give it back to the T Bar, all those people will have to go."

"I think I can tell which way you want me to rule."

She shrugged, striving to appear indifferent, with imperfect success. "You're the law. The only law around here, really. Ben Mackey's in Treadway's pocket. Treadway paid every cowboy and deadbeat to vote for Mackey. What did the cowboys care? They didn't want a strong sheriff anyway."

"Mackey's no longer sheriff of Valentine."

"Treadway won't like that. Or the fact that you killed one of his men and threw two more in the crossbars hotel. Be careful, Clay. Watch your back. Treadway is bad enough. But he's got a few more gunslingers on his payroll that you haven't met yet. One's the Cimarron Kid."

"The Cimarron Kid." Torn's eyes narrowed. "No, I've never met him. But I hear he's a fast draw."

"One of the fastest."

Torn finished his drink, set the shot glass down.

"Thanks for the bourbon, Rose. And the information."

"Is there anything else I can do for you?"

She said it with soft sincerity, and the offer caught Torn flatfooted. He hesitated. She was hurt by his hesitation, misconstruing it.

"Well," she said curtly, heading for the doors to the hallway. "I've got a business to run. Come see me some time, Clay. I . . ." She shook her head and left the parlor quickly, without a backward glance.

The Oriental girl reappeared with his hat and gun belt and showed him out. Torn stepped into the night feeling oddly despondent, like the poker player who folds with a hand that would have won the pot.

CHAPTER 10

TORN RETURNED TO THE JAIL TO CHECK ON HIS PRISONERS. All was quiet there, so he went on down the street to the Blue Chip Restaurant for supper. He was working on his dessert of apple cobbler and coffee when Joshua Quarles found him.

"Mind if I sit down?" asked the cattleman.

Torn motioned to the chair across the table. "Time for that talk you said we'd have?"

Quarles smiled. "I just want to make sure you understand my position."

"I'm listening," said Torn, and kept eating.

Quarles looked around the dining room. There were a half-dozen other patrons, and they all watched the corner table where Torn and Quarles were seated.

"Heard about your shoot-out at the Bull's-eye," said Quarles. "So has everyone else in town, I think."

"Good news travels fast."

"Rumor is you started the trouble. Folks here in Valentine are law-abiding. And they're disappointed in you. They were expecting a federal judge to ride in here and put a stop to the violence. Instead, you seem to add to it."

"Came to lecture me?"

Quarles had to make an effort to keep his smile firmly in place. "Not at all, Judge."

"I've heard a rumor, too. I've heard you and Olin Treadway are in cahoots."

Quarles was startled. "Where did you hear such a thing?"

"Doesn't matter. Is it true?"

"I know him," replied Quarles, noncommittal.

"Tell me about him."

"He was born in New York City. Worked as a roustabout and a strike-buster in his youth. The story goes his knack for breaking heads and busting knee-caps led to a murder charge. So he came west under a cloud. Like a whole lot of other men. He worked on the railroad for a while, the Union Pacific. Reached the position of crew foreman, but then he beat a naddy half to death for calling him a bastard, and the UP let him go. He went to work as a barkeep and bouncer after that, from one saloon and cathouse to the next. I have a suspicion that one night he bounced some luckless soul so hard a fat roll of banknotes fell out of the poor man's pocket, because somehow Treadway suddenly had enough greenbacks to buy his own place. They say you make your own luck in this world."

"Now he owns most of Keno Street."

"Happens to some men who go from rags to riches,

you know. They're haunted by memories of the days when they lived hand to mouth, and they never seem to have enough. They always want more. Like they're trying to put as much distance between themselves and poverty as possible."

"Same apply to you? I'm told you want to own all of the graze in Cherry County."

"Not really."

"But you want the T Bar. And if you own the T Bar and your own spread, well, that's a mighty big chunk of the county right there."

"There's no law against that, is there?"

"Depends on how you go about it."

"I'm not like Lane Terrill. I don't settle things with a gun. My men aren't the ones riding roughshod over the farmers."

"Not too long ago, down in Texas, I dealt with a man who wanted to be the big augur in his neck of the woods. He didn't believe in settling things with a gun, either. Instead, he partnered up with a Mexican bandit who did his dirty work for him."

"What happened to this man?" asked Quarles, like he already knew.

"I did. Did you warn those farmers what to expect from Terrill when you gave them that disputed land?"

"I sold it to them. Fair and square."

"Knowing all along what Lane Terrill would do."

His smile turning crafty, Quarles gave Torn a long, speculative look. He leaned forward, hands flat on the table.

"Lane and I agreed to make the Rosebud River the boundary between our two ranches. It's all on record, with our marks affixed. Legally, seems to me, it's cut and dried. It's not where the Rosebud was last year, or where it might run next year, but where it is today that marks the boundary line. So that *disputed* land, as you call it, is mine, and I passed clear title to those grangers."

"You want to know how I'm going to rule."

"Well." Quarles shrugged. "You have to admit, I have a vested interest."

"I'd say. If I rule that land is still T Bar property you've got to settle with the farmers."

"I can do that. And would, of course."

"Yes, you would," said Torn. "I'd make sure of that."

"Now, Judge," admonished Quarles. "You're trying to start more trouble."

"I can't stomach men who fight the way you do, Quarles."

"And how is that?"

"Underhanded."

"So you believe the rumors."

"They suit you." Torn finished his coffee, tossed his napkin on the table, and rose. Fishing a silver dollar out of his pocket, he put it on the table.

"I'm glad we had this little talk," said Quarles. "Now allow me to give you some advice. Let those two men out of jail."

"Treadway's men."

"Let them out. Or better yet, to make it nice and legal, set bail for them and Treadway will buy them out."

"Nice and legal," echoed Torn dryly. "That's the way you like everything."

"I have no personal interest in the release of those two men, understand. It is merely a matter of civic concern. I would like to see further bloodshed avoided, if possible. What are you holding them for? What charges have you brought against them?"

"They're hired killers," said Torn. "So is the owner of this." He brandished the Remington Navy from under his coat.

Across the dining room a woman gasped. A dropped fork clattered on the rim of a plate. Then the restaurant fell deathly silent.

Quarles didn't even twitch.

"You're going to have a bad reputation around here, Judge, if you keep acting like this."

"I figure there's a connection between those boys in jail and the man who lost this shooting iron. Who, with three others, tried to kill young Andy Terrill yesterday. Now, who would want Lane Terrill's son and only heir six feet under, Mister Quarles?"

The cattle baron's black eyes glittered, cold as the smile he managed to maintain.

"I said it before, Judge. I don't believe in settling differences with a gun. Unlike you."

"Sometimes it's the only way," said Torn, putting away the gun. He took his hat from the back of the chair he had just vacated, put it on and, turning briskly on his heel, walked out of the restaurant.

CHAPTER

11

TORN HEADED BACK TO THE HOTEL. IT WAS LATE. VALEN-
tine was quiet. Halfway to the Plainsman he faltered in
his resolve and bent his steps in the direction of Keno
Street, his thoughts hostage to Rose Pendergast. For
reasons he could not fully fathom, they had not parted
on the best of terms, and he was afraid of losing her
friendship. He didn't have so many friends that he
could afford to throw one away.

Something had come between them, and by the
time he reached the other side of Main Street he knew
what that something was. Or rather, who. Melony
Hancock. He felt the shape and weight of the daguerreotype in the pocket of his frock coat. He pulled
up short in the night shadows of a boardwalk fronting
a general store, cursing under his breath.

There was a special attraction between him and

Rose—he had felt it the first time they'd met. At the time she had been running a house of ill repute in Dodge. What she did for a living made no difference to him. He thought they were kindred spirits, in a way. Knew, all too well, how the quirky circumstances of life could force a man—or a woman—to do things they would not have chosen to do, had they been given the luxury of choice. All he had to do was look at himself to know this was true. He was living proof. Yes, Rose was a calico queen, but he did not look down on her for it, or think himself better than she.

She was in love with him, and therein lay the problem. Because he could not return that love. Not as long as he held to the memory of Melony Hancock. Tonight he wanted company. He was feeling lonesome. It happened. And she would welcome him with open arms. One less night alone. But it wasn't fair to her. He would be taking advantage of her feelings for him, and in the end he would ride away.

So he turned back, crossing the street to the Plainsman. In a bleak frame of mind, he scarcely noticed that there was no one at the desk. He climbed the stairs. The second-floor hallway was dark. Someone had forgotten to light the wall lamp. He thought nothing of it. There was a window at the end of the hall, a rectangle of gray gloom in the inky blackness.

His thoughts were still on Rose—he was prepared for them to remain on her for the duration of a long and sleepless night. But there was no way to distract the subconscious. An alarm went off in his head. He could smell a pungent trace of burnt tobacco—someone had recently smoked a roll-your-own in the hallway. Then, the creak of a door hinge behind him and, a second later, the faintest whisper of cloth. He was reaching for the Colt Peacemaker before he even thought about it. The instinct for self-preservation was taking over. Crouching, turning toward the sounds, he saw shadows move and separate in front of him, and knew then that there were two of them.

The man behind him had come out of the room adjacent to his. Torn saw the glimmer of a gun barrel being swept down at his skull with frightening speed. He threw his left arm up to deflect the blow. The gun barrel struck him high in the shoulder, on the bone, and the force behind the blow knocked him off balance. The exquisite pain made him gasp. He caught himself, still turning. The Colt cleared his holster, but before he could bring it to bear, the second man—the one who had been lurking in the dark corner of the hallway near the window, came up and struck him at the base of the skull with the barrel of his pistol. White hot agony exploded in Torn's head. He fell, half-conscious, his world spinning out of control. One of the men kicked him viciously in the ribs. Torn sprawled, the wind knocked out of him. The Colt slipped out of his grasp and clattered across the floor. He rolled over, dry-heaving, trying to get up, but he couldn't get his balance.

"Tough sonuvabitch," growled one of his attackers, begrudging admiration. "Let's kill him and be done with it."

"No," said the other. "I won't kill a man unless it's in a fair fight."

Torn, on hands and knees, groped blindly for the Remington Navy under his coat. He never touched it. The first speaker stepped in and pistol-whipped him again. This time the explosion of white agony was followed by black nothingness.

* * *

When he came to, sunlight was streaming through a window, and he watched the dust motes dance in the pale golden beam. Momentarily disoriented, he suddenly remembered the pistol-whipping, and his first reaction was to sit up quickly, alarmed. Pain seared through his skull and down his spine to course through his entire body. Gasping, he lay back down, squeezing his eyes tightly shut, fighting against the wave of black oblivion which threatened to sweep him away.

"Don't try to move, Clay."

His eyes snapped open, filled with surprise.

Rose Pendergast was leaning over him. Her golden hair was done up with jeweled hairpins. She was clad in a very respectable brown serge dress with yellow piping and lace at the cuffs and severely high collar.

"Where am I?" he croaked.

"Your hotel room."

"She's been sitting up with you all night," said Doc Wingate, appearing on the other side of the bed from Rose. "When I left here last night she was here, and she was still here when I came back this morning to check on you."

Rose smiled. "Think my reputation will be ruined when the good folks of Valentine find out I spent the night in a man's room?"

"It would seem you do have one friend in town, after all, Judge," said Wingate, checking Torn's pulse against his Ingersoll keywinder. "Do you remember what happened?"

"Yes."

"That's a good sign."

"I think there were two of them. Waiting in the hall."

"You have a thick skull. You came away with only a mild concussion."

Torn touched the dressing bound tightly around his head. He was lying on top of the bed covers. His shirt was off. There was a livid bruise on his left side, where the attacker had kicked him.

"It appears they tried to crack a few of your ribs, too," remarked Wingate. "As best I can tell, they failed. You must lead a violent life, Judge. I don't think I've ever seen so many scars on one man."

"Who found me?" asked Torn.

Wingate glanced across at Rose.

"I did," said Rose, firing a defiant look right back at the sawbones. "I think it must have just happened when I came up."

Torn smiled. "Funny, I was thinking about coming to see you last night, Rose."

"If you had," said Wingate, clearing his throat, "you might have missed out on a lot of pain."

Heartache is pain, thought Torn.

"You were thinking about coming to see me," said Rose. "But you didn't. I doubted that you would. That's why I . . ." She glanced sharply at Wingate. "What?"

Wingate was suppressing a smile, with mediocre success. "Nothing, ma'am."

Torn got the impression Wingate liked Rose. Which was a mark in the doctor's favor.

"I wonder why they didn't kill me when they had the chance?" mused Torn.

"I believe they were after the keys to the jail," said Wingate. "Apparently, your prisoners escaped during the night."

"Have you treated any other gunslingers besides Booth in the last few days?"

Wingate frowned. "What do you mean?"

"I shot two men who were trying to kill Andy Terrill less than a day's ride west of here, near the road to Cody. If they needed a doctor, is there anyone else in Cherry County besides you?"

"No, there isn't," said Wingate. "And no I haven't."

"Would you tell me if you had?"

"Probably not. That would lead to more shooting."

"They're bad men, Doc. On the wrong side of the law."

"Are they? Because you say they're on the wrong side?"

"What side are you on?"

"On the side of live and let live." Wingate snapped his medical grip shut. "I recommend you stay in bed for at least a couple of days. Head injuries are not to be taken lightly."

"How much do I owe you?"

Wingate glanced at Rose again. "It's taken care of." He left the room.

Torn tried sitting up again, slowly this time. He sat on the edge of the bed a moment, breathing gingerly, and waiting for his head to explode. The room spun, and he felt nauseous.

"The doctor said you should stay in bed, Clay," said Rose.

"Too much to do."

"How about if I stay in bed with you? Would that change your mind?"

He smiled back at her. "It's tempting."

"But not tempting enough."

"Rose . . ."

"You don't have to explain."

"I ought to. I owe you . . ."

"You don't owe me anything."

Uncomfortable, Torn changed the subject. "I owe you the doctor's fee. Unless they took my money, too."

"Your money's on the table over there."

Torn pushed off the bed and stood a moment, testing his equilibrium. Once he was fairly sure he wouldn't fall flat on his face, he walked, very slowly, across the room. On top of the table next to the window was his gun belt with the Colt Peacemaker, the shoulder rig with the saber knife, a thin roll of greenbacks, and Melony's daguerreotype.

"I had another pistol on me," he said. "A Remington Navy with notches in the grip."

She shook her head.

Torn nodded grimly. "It figures."

"She was very pretty," said Rose.

Torn gazed at the daguerreotype. An invisible fist punched him in the guts—always did when he looked at the photograph.

"I'd bet she still is," he said.

"It just makes me want to cry," said Rose. She was angry with herself. "And I haven't cried since I was a child. It seems like such a waste."

"What does?"

"You. Spending your whole life looking for her. Clay, we find love and we lose it. That's all part of life. You've got to learn to let go when it's time, even though it hurts when you give up. Believe me, I know how hard it is. But you have to let go, and make room in your heart for new love when it comes."

Torn gazed out the window at Valentine's bustling main street.

"You make a lot of sense, Rose," he said eventually. "And I'm not really sure what it is inside me that won't let go."

"She must have been a wonderful person, and I'm sure you loved her with all your heart. And I think, if she knew what you were putting yourself through on her account she'd want you to let go and start all over with your life."

He sighed. "It gets me through the days—the chance that maybe tomorrow I'll find her."

He dared to look at her then, and saw what he had been most afraid of seeing. Her indigo eyes were wet with tears.

"I'm sorry," he said.

"Sorry," she echoed, bitter. "You've been riding in and out of my life for years, Clay. I lied when I said I hadn't cried since I was a child. I cry every time you ride away. And I hate it. I hate it!"

"Then take your own advice," he said gently. "Forget about me. Let it go."

"Yes. I suppose I will," she whispered, turning away. "Even though it hurts so much to do so."

He heard the door shut, didn't turn around. Standing at the window, he watched her cross the street, still muddy from yesterday's downpour.

Then he put on a clean shirt, buckled on gun belt and shoulder rig. Donning hat and coat, he left the hotel and made his way to the Bull's-eye Saloon.

CHAPTER 12

It was a little early for saloon business, and the Bull's-eye was almost empty. The chairs were overturned on top of the deal tables. The only person in the place was Patch, the obstreperous barkeep. He was behind the mahogany, filling bottles with watered-down rotgut, when Torn strolled in. The left side of his face was swollen and discolored, with a half-dozen cuts, where Torn had hit him with the bottle in yesterday's altercation. He glanced at Torn, did a double take. His eyes widened and then narrowed into hostile slits. He reached under the bar. Torn swept back his frock coat and laid hold of his Colt.

"If you're reaching for the sawed-off," he rasped, "think twice."

"You've got a lot of hard bark on you, mister," sneered Patch, "comin' back in here."

"I go where I want."

"Then go to hell," growled the surly codger. But he had apparently thought twice, and laid his hands on the top of the bar in plain view.

"I want to talk to Treadway."

"Here I am."

The man who emerged from the back room did not by his nature and looks seem to fit the brown broadcloth suit he wore as well as it fit him. His features were broad and pockmarked. His bushy eyebrows met at the bridge of his nose, a black ledge sheltering small, deep-set, furtive eyes. His nose had been broken a couple of times, a mishapen blob over a brutal, knife-slit mouth. He was broad across the chest and shoulders. His legs were short and stout. A big man—though no match for Grizzly in sheer bulk. A long-nine jutted from his teeth, smoldering, and when he reached up to pluck it out, Torn noticed the scarred knuckles. Treadway looked rough-hewn, and no hand-tailored suits would make him look otherwise. Torn recalled Rose saying that she was afraid of this man, and he could see why. Treadway looked like someone who enjoyed inflicting pain.

"What do you want?" asked Treadway, his voice harsh and gravelly. He sauntered past the hash counter and approached the bar.

"The two gunslingers I had locked up."

Treadway gestured, indicating the empty room. "You see 'em here? You're bad for business, Torn. Waltzing in here, shooting up the place. Where are your manners?"

"What kind of business is that, Treadway? The dry-gulching business?"

"Still making trouble." Treadway smirked. "How come you're so dead set on muddying up my water?"

"It's my job. It's what I do."

"I'm a law-abiding citizen of this fair town. You've got no call harassing me."

"What does a law-abiding citizen need with hired guns on his payroll?"

"This business can get rough. Cowboys are wild critters sometimes—a little too wild, often as not, when they get a bellyful of who-hit-john. Got to keep 'em in line. As you've seen, we don't have much of a sheriff here. So I hire my own protection."

"Not much of a sheriff." Torn laughed. "That was your doing."

"A rumor, and untrue. I didn't buy Mackey that badge. But you'd be surprised how effective men like Booth and Grizzly can be. They don't have to lift a finger to protect my property. Just be seen. Has a sobering effect on a wayward cowboy, I can tell you."

"So where are they now?"

"The tall timber, I reckon."

"You're saying you don't know," said Torn, with rank skepticism.

"I don't know," nodded Treadway. "I had nothing to do with the jailbreak." He flashed a meaningless smile. "You don't believe me. But you can't prove I did have anything to do with it, now can you? Maybe you'd like to throw me in jail."

"Maybe I ought to."

"On what charge?"

"Maybe you're wanted for murder back East."

"Another rumor. Also untrue. I have a hunch you're just fishing without a hook."

"And I have a hunch it was your men who jumped

me last night. And your men who ambushed Andy Terrill."

"Prove it."

"I will," said Torn. "Count on it."

He turned for the door.

"So all you came for was to threaten me," said Treadway, derisive.

"To give you fair warning," answered Torn, and walked out.

"Someone needs to take that pilgrim down a notch or two," growled Patch.

A second man stepped from the back room and walked over to the bar. He was young, rail-thin, with boyish features. A rattlesnake band adorned his flat-crowned hat, which hung down his back by the chin strap. He wore a red double-breasted shirt and black whipcord pants tucked into boots which sported big Chihuahua spurs. When he walked he dragged his heels so that the rowels sang against the floor. He liked to hear the jingle-jangle of his spurs.

"Speak of the devil," said Treadway, with a wry smile. "Here's a man who could do the job. The Cimarron Kid."

"I'd like a beer, please," said The Kid politely.

Patch drew the beer from a cask beneath the mahogany. He always felt a little funny serving The Kid, because The Kid looked too young to even set foot inside a saloon, much less indulge in strong drink.

"Of course, I could be wrong," continued Treadway, talking to Patch. "I say that because The Kid here had a chance to put Judge Torn in the local bone orchard, and didn't."

"I don't work like that, Mister Treadway," said The Kid calmly. "You know that."

"Yes." Treadway nodded emphatically. "Yes, I suppose I do."

"Fact is, I didn't much care for that business last night," said The Kid. "I don't like hiding in the shadows waiting to ambush a man."

"Well, we couldn't let Booth and Grizzly rot in jail, now could we?"

"No, sir. I reckon we couldn't, if you say so. To be honest, though, I really don't much care what happens to Booth and Grizzly."

He made the admission matter-of-factly, without rancor.

Treadway took the time to pick his next words with care. He respected The Kid's prowess with a gun. Behind that boyish, soft-spoken, faultlessly polite exterior lurked a born killer. A man who was arguably the fastest draw on the frontier. The Cimarron Kid had slain thirteen men in his brief career, and every one of them a fair fight. In fact, it was said The Kid let his adversary draw first every time. Even then, not one of The Kid's thirteen victims had gotten off a single shot. The Kid waited until the other man's gun had cleared the holster. Then he drew and fired—always before the other man could squeeze his pistol's trigger. And The Kid was a dead shot. He went either for the heart or right between the eyes, depending on how he felt that day. He never missed.

There was, thought Treadway, something arrogant in the way The Kid let his adversary draw first. And there was arrogance, too, in the way The Kid turned up his nose at men like Booth and Grizzly. Like he was somehow better than they were, and did not care to associate with the likes of them. Treadway suspected The Kid thought the same way about him, and that rankled. But The Cimarron Kid was one man Treadway didn't think he ought to aggravate. The scary thing about The Kid was that he didn't get mad. He didn't flare up when someone insulted him. There was no warning. The Kid would kill you without blinking an eye, and there was no telling what might trigger this homicidal impulse. Treadway did not want to be called out onto the gunman's sidewalk.

"Now, now, Kid," said Treadway. "They are your colleagues, after all. Maybe they're not as quick with a gun as you are, but you shouldn't hold that against them."

"I don't, Mister Treadway. I just don't care for back shooters. That goes for Farnum, double. Farnum would've plugged that judge last night. The man was down, and Farnum wanted to shoot him." The Kid shook his head in quiet disgust.

"I wish you had let him." Treadway sighed. "I have a bad feeling about Torn. He could make a lot of trouble. Scotch things up good."

The Kid sipped his beer, wiping foam from his upper lip with the back of his hand. "Well, Mister Treadway, you pay me my wage, so if you say call him out, I'll call him out."

"But you see, Kid, that wouldn't work in this case. You're linked to me. So if you gunned down a federal judge in the middle of the street at high noon in front of God and everybody, people would know I ordered you to do it."

"I see." The Kid nodded, sympathetic. "But what can he do? He doesn't know anything, and how could he find out?"

"What can he do? Well, he killed Preacher yesterday, and Quint the day before. You took Quint's gun from Torn?"

The Kid nodded, sipping his beer.

"He's got Booth and Sam Cherokee laid up, all shot to hell," continued Treadway. "I'd say Judge Torn is doing plenty. All I've got left is you and Farnum and Grizzly, and Grizzly has to lay low."

"The judge will never find Grizzly and Booth and that damned ole half-breed," declared Patch. "Them all tucked away in that line shack up on Dog Creek."

"Courtesy of Mister Joshua Quarles." Treadway chuckled.

"I say get Farnum to bushwhack the judge," suggested Patch. "He done a job on Lane Terrill, Farnum did. He can do the same for Torn."

Treadway glanced curiously at The Kid. The latter clearly disapproved of the barkeeper's proposal.

"Think maybe that's how it'll have to be," said Treadway, feigning reluctance. "You can see that, can't you, Kid?"

The Kid shrugged bony shoulders. "You're the boss."

"But first, I think Farnum ought to take care of Ben Mackey."

"The sheriff?" queried Patch. "How come?"

"It was Mackey who brought me that telegram Andy Terrill sent from Cody. Torn isn't the kind to leave any stone unturned. He knows something's going on here, and he's bound and bulldog determined to get to the bottom of it. Now, Mackey's a spineless sonuvabitch. He'll spill the beans if Torn leans on him." Treadway turned to The Kid again. "Where is Farnum, anyway?"

"The Yellow Rose, I think."

Patch grinned. "He does like the ladies, don't he?"

"Fetch him for me, Kid," said Treadway. "Tell him he's got work to do."

CHAPTER

13

TREADWAY HAD AT LEAST ONE THING GOING FOR HIM—HE was an extraordinary judge of character. He'd always had a knack for accurately sizing up a man, and then, putting himself in that man's shoes, anticipating what that man would do in response to circumstances. This knack had saved Treadway's bacon on more than one occasion during the course of his shady career.

In this case he pegged Torn correctly as a very thorough and resolute individual.

He would not have been surprised to know that, immediately after leaving the Bull's-eye Saloon, Torn went in search of Valentine's telegraph office.

"There was a telegram sent from Cody by Andy Terrill a few days ago," Torn informed the telegrapher.

The gaunt and gangly man behind the counter peered owlishly at Torn from beneath a green eyeshade. His Adam's apple bobbed in a spindly throat as he swallowed hard. Torn could sense the man's apprehension.

"I'll have to check my records," said the key operator.

"No you don't. You remember."

The Adam's apple was going great guns now. The telegrapher looked very much like a rabbit ready to run.

"You're . . . you're that federal judge been causing so much trouble 'round here, ain't you?"

Torn sighed. "The telegraph from Andy Terrill. You sent it on to the T Bar?"

"Sure. Billy Oates took it."

"Who is Billy Oates?"

"Young feller. Lives here in town. Pa's the blacksmith over at Kostmyer's Livery. Billy runs the telegrams out to the local spreads for me, when any come over the wire. I pay him four bits each ride. Got himself a fast horse. Paint pony. His pa bought it off a Kiowa buck last year for a bottle of snakehead. Billy calls himself the Paul Revere of Cherry County." The telegrapher tried a halfhearted grin at that, but when he saw no trace of amusement on Torn's stern, sundark features, the grin quickly died.

"That's fine," said Torn. "So you gave Billy Oates the telegram. Who else did you give it to?"

The key operator was blinking rapidly. "Nobody. Honest."

Torn leaned over the counter. The man shrank back.

"You're not telling me the truth," said Torn. His voice was low and laced with menace.

"Sheriff Mackey," blurted the telegrapher, fearing for his health and well-being. "Don't hurt me, mister."

Torn's smile was cold. "My bad reputation is good for something."

Crestfallen, the man said, "Sheriff told me to let him know when anything concerning the T Bar came over the wire."

"You could lose your job for doing that."

"He's the sheriff," protested the man.

"Not any longer."

"He told me it was okay. Said he was investigatin' Lane Terrill, on account of all the night riding those T Bar cowboys were doing to try and drive those homesteaders off the Rosebud."

Torn left the telegraph office without bothering to thank the key operator. He walked on down Main to the edge of town, and asked Kostmyer where Ben Mackey lived.

"If he isn't at the Bull's-eye you'll like as not find him in his room at the hotel," said the livery owner. "In a drunken stupor, no doubt." He seemed to feel it was his duty to disparage everyone he talked about in some form or fashion.

Torn was climbing the steps of the Plainsman's boardwalk when Mackey emerged from the lobby. Valentine's ex-sheriff was stumbling a little. He reeked of cheap whiskey. His nose had been set and bandaged. Blinded by the brightness of the day, he didn't see Torn until it was too late. He bumped into Torn. Anticipating the collision, Torn lowered his shoulder and sent Mackey reeling. Mackey careened against a bench backed up against the clapboard wall of the hotel, banging his leg against it. Making incoherent noises, he tried to run. Torn tripped him up, and

Mackey landed hard, face-first. He bellowed in pain, and when he rolled over on his back Torn saw blood spotting the bandage on his nose.

The humiliation was too much for Ben Mackey. Long dormant pride welled up inside him. Torn had bullied him past all endurance. He slapped leather, going for his six-gun. Torn kicked it out of his grasp. The gun sailed into the street. Torn reached down to gather handfuls of Mackey's shirt. He hauled the man to his feet. Mackey swung at him. This sudden and unexpected display of backbone startled Torn. Fortunately, the blow was poorly aimed, glancing off Torn's jaw. Torn hurled Mackey off the boardwalk. The ex-badge-toter bounced off a tie rail and landed in a horse trough full of rainwater.

"What's happening here?" shrilled the hotel desk clerk, running out of the lobby.

"Get back inside," rasped Torn.

The desk clerk turned tail.

Mackey was floundering in the horse trough, splashing water everywhere. Torn stepped in and fished him out.

"Who did you tell about Andy Terrill coming in alone from Cody?" asked Torn.

Mackey spluttered, making a noise that was half growl and half whine.

Torn's head was throbbing mercilessly. He was not in a tolerant frame of mind. He shook Mackey hard enough to rattle teeth.

"You set Andy Terrill up for a dry gulching," he snapped. "You as much as signed his death warrant. Who did you tell? It was Treadway, wasn't it? It was four of Treadway's hired killers who waylaid Andy Terrill."

"I won't tell you nothing!" screamed Mackey.

Torn spun him around and bent him over the horse trough, holding Mackey's head and shoulders underwater. He counted to ten and let the man up for air. Mackey wheezed and choked and struggled in vain.

"You're going to come clean, Mackey," said Torn.

"He'll kill me!" gasped Mackey. "I can't . . ."

Torn dunked him again. This time he counted to fifteen. When Mackey came back up he let out a bloodcurdling howl.

"Talk," rasped Torn.

He was vaguely aware of people coming from both ends of the street. Some were walking, others were running, drawn by the commotion in front of the Plainsman. He paid them scant attention. He was focused on getting the truth out of Mackey. If he could persuade the ex-law dog to implicate Treadway then the deal was done. Torn could make out a warrant for Treadway's arrest and serve it personally. All he needed was a confession from Mackey, and while he didn't particularly enjoy getting that confession by such means as this, he sensed it was no time for niceties.

So he wasn't expecting it when someone jumped him from behind—someone who tried to hook Torn's arms, hoping to break Torn's hold on Mackey. Torn let the ex-sheriff go and whirled, shaking the attacker loose.

Doc Wingate slammed against a boardwalk upright. Torn had an arm cocked back for a swing when he recognized the gray-haired sawbones.

"Go ahead," said Wingate. "What are you waiting for? Hit me. Hell, Judge, why don't you just shoot me?"

Torn lowered his arm, glanced around. A crowd had

gathered—a circle of scowling faces and hostile mutterings.

"You're no better than the men you stand against," declared Wingate. "You use the law as a license."

"He just jumped me!" complained Mackey. "You all are witnesses. He started beating me for no good reason. Then he damn near drowned me!"

"Get out of Valentine!" someone growled from the crowd.

"Yeah, we don't need your kind of law and order," said another.

"Git while you can," warned a third.

The bullet splintered the upright inches from Doc Wingate's head, a fraction of a second before the gunshot rolled across the heat-hammered street.

The crowd scattered like a covey of quail flushed out of shinnery. Torn lunged, carrying Wingate down onto the boardwalk. He rolled over, drawing the Colt Peacemaker, and saw Mackey standing there, frozen by fear.

"Get down!" yelled Torn.

The second bullet slammed into Mackey's back and blew a big bloody hole in his chest.

He stood a second longer, staring stupidly at Torn, before pitching violently forward. His upper body thumped against the edge of the boardwalk.

Calculating the angle of the killing shot, Torn jumped up and scanned the rooftops across the street. He thought he saw a wisp of gunsmoke above the roofline of the general store. But he couldn't be sure. He didn't feel too sure about anything—except that his best, and maybe his only, chance to stop Treadway lay dead at his feet.

CHAPTER 14

TORN RETRIEVED HIS CLAYBANK FROM KOSTMYER'S LIVERY,
crossed the Niobrara on the ferry, and rode past the
grave of Lane Terrill in the shade of Two Mile Pine on
his way to the T Bar ranch.

This proved to be a rambling affair fashioned from
big pine logs, and Torn figured a great deal of sweat
and toil had gone into hauling that timber from the
woodlands which lay several days ride west. In addi-
tion to the main house there was a barn, two bunk-
houses, a half-dozen corrals and breaking pens, and a
variety of outbuildings.

He was still a good quarter mile from the place
when he heard a rider behind him. Considering the
events of the past few days, he braced for trouble,
checking the claybank and resting his hand on the
holstered Colt Peacemaker.

But the rider wasn't much interested in him. He galloped past Torn on an apron-faced sorrel, blistering the hayburner with his quirt. A T Bar cowboy, guessed Torn. The range rider yelled something at Torn as he flashed by, but Torn couldn't make it out. Whatever news he bore, he was in an all-fired hurry to get it delivered. Bad news, probably. Torn kicked the claybank into a canter and followed in the cowboy's wake.

By the time he reached the big house, there was a congregation of cowboys gathered on the hard pack out in front. The cowboy who had humped his tail past Torn moments earlier was the center of attention. He was talking up to Andy Terrill, who stood on the porch of the main house looking grim. The messenger's jiggered horse stood, lathered and slay-legged, with its head down, all tuckered out. The cowboy had clearly come a long way in a short time.

When he saw Torn, Andy stepped down off the porch and made his way through the press of T Bar hands to meet him.

"What happened?" asked Torn.

"Someone slaughtered a bunch of T Bar cattle," said Andy. He sounded more baffled than irate.

"Where?"

"Over near the Rosebud."

"Them squatters done it," opined one of the cowboys.

"Damned churn-twisters," grumbled another.

"What do you think?" Andy asked Torn.

"I wouldn't be surprised. Getting back at you for what happened to Caldwell."

Andy looked around at the cowboys. They were watching him like a passel of hawks. Torn figured they were all waiting to see what their new boss would do. It was the moment of truth, for them and for Andy. What Andy did now would color all his future dealings with these men. Torn could see that the young Terrill was on the horns of a dilemma. Apparently, so could Jericho Gentry, who came forward to confront Andy.

"What are you going to do about this, Mister Terrill?" asked the black top hand.

Andy glanced up at Torn.

"I know what your pa woulda done," declared Dusty Burcham, also stepping forward. "You can't let them get away with this."

Torn felt sympathy for Andy. The young man had yet to prove himself to these men, and it was in the cards that he would have to sooner or later. If he didn't live up to their expectations, most, if not all, of the hands would probably pack their possibles, saddle their cayuses, and make dust. And, assuming Andy intended to run the T Bar, he needed cowboys to make a go of it.

"We better go take a look," said Torn.

"Yes." Andy nodded, resigned. "I suppose we better do just that."

Dusty turned to the rest of the outfit.

"Saddle up, boys," he called eagerly.

"Wait a minute," said Torn. "We don't need the whole crew."

Dusty glowered. "Who's running this show?"

"If they're killing T Bar cattle," said Jericho calmly, "they might not blink at killing another Terrill."

"Very well," said Andy. "Jericho, you and Dusty and . . . three others." He looked up at Torn again, and Torn nodded. That seemed to be a workable compromise. "Judge, will you come inside for a minute? I'd like a word with you."

"I'll pick you out a good mount, Mister Terrill," said Dusty.

Once through the front door of the big house, Torn found himself in a long room incorporating some big pieces of age-blackened furnishings and a fireplace large enough to burn a cord of wood in all at once. Andy stood in the middle of the room, hands on hips, staring for a long stretch at a framed map of Cherry County on the wall above the mantel. The T Bar was emphasized in a dull red that looked like an old bloodstain on the parchment. It seemed to Torn as though the spacious room kind of swallowed up Andy Terrill.

"It makes no sense to me," said Andy plaintively. "Why would they kill cattle?"

"Striking back. They're scared. Scared men do stupid things. They figure they're at war with the T Bar Ranch."

"I don't want to fight a war."

"You aim to hold onto this place?"

Andy took a moment before answering. "I don't know if I can."

"A person can do whatever he makes up his mind to do. The question wasn't whether you can, but whether you want to."

"I haven't made up my mind. What about you, Judge? Have you made a decision about the disputed land?"

"I think the farmers ought to stay."

"So you'll rule against the T Bar."

"It isn't personal. Your father agreed to make the Rosebud his boundary line. It still is."

Andy nodded. "I have no quarrel with that. There's plenty of land to go around."

"Glad to hear you say that. There are some who don't see it that way."

"You mean those men out there."

"They've been through hell and high water for your father. They don't give their loyalty easily. It takes a special breed of man to earn their trust. But once they give it, it's given for good. They don't know you. But they know what Lane Terrill would do."

"Maybe my father was wrong this time. Don't they consider that? Don't they realize those farmers have certain rights, too?"

"They'll have nothing good to say about farmers, Andy. They don't understand farming. It's a concept that's foreign to them. They hate to see the open range plowed up and turned over. It's a threat to their very way of life, and to their way of thinking, that way is the only way worth living.

"Your biggest problem is that those cowboys believe one of the farmers killed your father, a man they loved and respected. They aren't inclined to let that go."

"But all those homesteaders can't be held responsible for what one man did."

If Caldwell really killed Lane Terrill, thought Torn. He kept that thought to himself.

"Those men out there won't buy that argument," he said.

"So there will be more killing," said Andy in despair. "My God, some of those men rode out and grabbed Caldwell and hanged him! No one knows for sure if it was Caldwell who killed my father. We may never know for sure who did. But that didn't make any difference to the men who stretched his neck."

"We may know the truth before this is finished."

Andy didn't seem to hear. "They might have murdered an innocent man. The thing is, we'll never find out which of them did the deed. You realize that, don't you, Judge? They're a clannish bunch, that crew."

Torn heard horses outside. A moment later, Dusty barged in.

"We're ready to ride."

Andy started for the door.

"You better go heeled," advised Dusty.

"What?"

"He's right," said Torn grimly. "You better take a gun. And I don't mean that peashooter I saw you with the other day."

"So you believe there will be gunplay," said Andy. "I thought your job was to keep the peace."

"I'll do what I can. But they might start shooting before I can talk sense into them."

Andy went to the gun case and removed a Henry repeater. Holding the rifle awkwardly, he said, "I don't like this. I don't intend to shoot anybody."

"I know," replied Torn. "You didn't start this fight, but you're in it now up to your neck, and you may have to finish it."

"You have to do something."

Torn's smile was self-deprecating. "Well, I've been trying. Can't say I've had much success so far."

For the first time, Andy noticed Torn's bandages. But before he could comment on them, Dusty spoke up.

"We're burning daylight," complained the hot-tempered cowboy. "Reckon you all could wait until later to play all this chin music?"

"Let's go." Andy sighed, and walked out.

"Dusty," said Torn.

The redheaded range rider drew up short.

"If you start using that charcoal-burner of yours, it better be in self-defense."

Dusty flashed a wicked grin. "Don't try to short-rein me, Judge. It'll be bad medicine if you do."

CHAPTER 15

THEY DIDN'T REALLY NEED THE LINE RIDER WHO HAD brought them word of the cattle killing to lead them back to the scene. Not far from the Rosebud, and still miles away from the carnage, they saw a dense black moving cloud hovering in the clear and brassy sky. Closer, they discovered that the cloud was in fact scores of turkey vultures.

"Must be every danged buzzard in Cherry County come to this feed," commented Dusty.

There were many more of the scavengers on the ground, feeding off the bloated carcasses of the dead cattle. Torn and the others paused on the rim of the hollow where the massacre had occurred. They saw empty shell casings on the ground—a lot of them, glinting in the harsh late afternoon sunlight. Plenty of tracks, too, the sign of men and mounts. Checking the lay of the land, Torn figured the men who had done the deed had encircled the hollow, dismounted, and had themselves a shooting spree, firing down into the trapped cattle from all sides.

He counted fifty-seven carcasses, every one of them swarmed by the turkey vultures. It was not a pretty sight. The buzzards fought for space and plucked bloody chunks of meat out of the slaughtered beeves, ripping open the tough cowhide with their sharp beaks.

One of the T Bar cowboys, whose name Torn had learned was Lem, drew his saddle gun. Everyone present surmised his intention was to bag as many of the good-for-nothing buzzards as possible. Another man, whose name Torn did not know, thought that was a splendid idea, and drew his own repeater from its scabbard. Torn kicked the claybank forward and then turned it across their line of fire as they lifted the rifles to their shoulders.

"Save your ammunition," he told them.

"He's right," said Jericho. "It was a passel of farmers who done this." He was studying the sign with a frown.

"But it was done this morning," said Dusty. "Those plow pushers are long gone. Back to their middle-busters, tearin' up the range. I say we go pay them a visit."

"We don't want any shooting," said Andy.

"Who says?" Dusty peered at him defiantly. "What do you reckon they did here? They did some shooting. They shot you out of a lot of money, *Mister* Terrill. Twenty dollars a head you could have gotten for those beeves at railhead. So that comes to . . . to . . ."

The effort at ciphering produced a scowl of mental agony on Dusty's face.

"Eleven hundred and forty dollars," said Andy.

"Why, that would pay my wage for a couple of years," declared Dusty, hoping to drive his point home.

"Three years, actually, at thirty dollars a month," corrected Andy, off the cuff. "With a little change left over."

"And you're gonna let 'em get away with it? Your father would've . . ."

"My father is dead," snapped Andy, with a vehemence that surprised everyone. "Precisely because he tried to settle things with bullets."

"So why'd we come all the way out here?" queried Dusty, aggravated, "if we aren't going to do anything about this?"

Andy looked soberly at Torn. "I think we had better try to talk it out with those farmers. If we don't at least try to settle our differences peacefully, then it won't be just cattle getting killed next time."

"Your memory's shorter than flea hair," snapped Dusty. "A man's already been killed. Your father."

"I know that," Andy snapped right back. "And you're forgetting Caldwell. He's dead, too. Remember? Perhaps you were there when it happened."

Dusty's lean features were drawn and flush with anger. He looked to be a long mile past the point of being ready for a fight.

"You got no right to . . ." he began.

"To talk to you in that manner? You are quite mistaken, Mister Burcham. I do have the right. I am your employer. And if you do not like the way I talk to you, or the way I choose to run this ranch, you are free to resign your position."

"Resign my position?" spluttered Dusty, affronted.

"Reckon he means you can quit," drawled Lem, laconic.

Dusty looked at Jericho, like he couldn't believe his ears. Andy glanced again at Torn, abashed. No one was more startled than he by this audacious and totally out-of-character display of decisive authority. Torn was pleased, and beginning to think he had grievously misjudged Andy Terrill. The young man was possessed of hidden qualities he would need to see him through the present difficulties.

"Let's go find those farmers," said Andy, none too enthusiastic over the prospect.

"Don't need to," remarked Jericho, almost casually. "I think they found us."

Torn looked sharply at Jericho, then followed the black cowboy's gaze to the rim on the other side of the hollow. More than a dozen men had appeared in a line on their mules and plow mares. At a distance of less than a hundred yards, he could tell with certainty that they were farmers by their dress and their weapons. They carried a variety of hardware: old thumb busters, shotguns, hunting rifles. Almost in unison, they dismounted and began shooting.

Most of the lead they were slinging fell harmlessly short. Most, but not all. Torn heard a wheezing grunt and knew before looking that one of the T Bar men had been hit. It was Lem. He slumped forward over the neck of his horse, and would have slipped sideways to the ground had Jericho not reached out to catch him and hold him in the saddle.

What followed was mass confusion. The buzzards

which had been feeding on the carcasses of the dead cattle winged skyward, their feasting disturbed. Several of them were killed as they rose from the ground into the line of fire. Dusty and another cowboy drew their saddle guns and began shooting back. Torn couldn't blame them. When it came to survival, you put right and wrong aside. He couldn't tell if the return fire had much effect. A pall of gray-white gunsmoke obscured the skirmish line of homesteaders.

Torn remained the calmest of the lot. His war experience was to thank for that. He had the ability to stay calm under enemy fire. As a result he was able to think clearly, and act sensibly where other men only reacted.

He realized that the farmers had been laying in wait, and he had to admire the strategy they had employed. Killing the cattle had not been merely a case of senseless payback, after all. In that respect he had underestimated them. They had been counting on the slaughter of T Bar beeves to bring instant retaliation down upon their heads, and they had done it to draw into ambush the T Bar riders they believed had been terrorizing them all this time.

He also realized that the farmers, in general, were probably better shots than the cowboys who were riding with him. The farmer had to be a hunter as well. As a rule, he had grown up going out with long rifle or shotgun to bag game to put meat on his table. In the process, he had developed into a good shot, because to be anything less would waste expensive powder and shot, and he was nothing if not frugal.

The same could not be said of the average cowboy. Some were fair shots, others downright sorry ones. A precious few had any real gun-handling ability. The best were usually those who plied their trade on ranches in areas where rustlers and hostile Indians were a problem. For that reason, in Torn's opinion, Texas range riders were generally a cut above the rest. They worked where the threat of Comanche and Mexican bandit depredations were constant.

Torn figured the only advantage he and the T Bar crew had in their favor was distance. The farmers could shoot like the dickens, and they had the element of surprise in their favor, but the quality of their weapons betrayed them. They had sprung the trap with daring, but it wasn't a tight enough trap—the range was too great for shotgun accuracy, and most of their rifles were old single-shot breechloaders, a fact which cut down severely on rate of fire.

For that reason he called a retreat.

Only Dusty Burcham seemed opposed to the idea. The other cowboys were too shocked by the aggression of the farmers to object. Torn knew that, given time to think, they would hate themselves for running from a bunch of plow pushers, but none of them was sufficiently cool and collected to think at the moment. So they paid heed to Torn's sharp-spoken command. As an ex-cavalry commander, he had learned how to pitch his voice above gun thunder.

Everyone but Dusty turned tail. Burcham sat his dancing horse and kept firing his Winchester. He was shooting too fast, and on horseback, to have much effect.

Torn yelled at him to give it up as he sped by on the long-legged claybank, following Andy and the others in flight.

He didn't much care for running, either. But he had a hunch the farmers would fall for an old cavalry tactic and give chase, thinking they had the day won. Torn almost wished they wouldn't. Because then the tables would turn. He would find ground of his own choosing, heel around suddenly, and give them the fight they were looking for.

Ahead of him, he saw Andy check and turn his horse. Andy was looking past him, at the rim of the hollow they had just quit. The expression on young Terrill's face caused Torn to stop the claybank and look back himself.

Dusty's horse was down, shot.

And Dusty was pinned to the ground, his leg trapped under almost a half ton of dying horse.

"Damn!" breathed Torn.

Next he knew, Andy was galloping past him, kicking his horse back up to the rim.

"Andy, wait!"

But Andy did not seem to hear him.

Without second thought, Torn spun the claybank around, drawing the Winchester 44/40 out of its saddle boot as he rode hell-bent for election back into the storm of hot lead.

CHAPTER 16

DUSTY BURCHAM CURSED A BLUE STREAK.

His cayuse had suffered a mortal wound, but it wasn't dead yet. It had dropped so suddenly that Dusty had been unable to kick boot out of stirrup and jump free. In the fall he had lost his hold on the Winchester "Yellow Boy" with which he had been blasting away at the farmers, and now the repeater lay tantalizingly just out of reach. Worse, the horse in its death throes had twisted just so, and in horror Dusty had felt the bone in his right leg fracture midway between knee and ankle. Heard it crack, too, clear as a bell. It wasn't the first bone Dusty had broken. In his opinion, every cowboy worth his salt had broken something or other. But that didn't make the pain any easier to bear. If not for cowboy pride, Dusty would have screamed in agony. Instead, he swore.

Worst of all, the farmers were coming.

Seeing Torn and the other T Bar riders flee, the homesteaders had jumped back aboard their mules and plow mares and barreled across the hollow. A few of them kept shooting as they rode. Dusty's body was twisted so that he lay on his right side, with his side gun under him, poking him in the kidney. When he tried to turn his body so that he could get to the gun, waves of searing pain left him gasping and dizzy, drenched with a cold sweat, and almost too afraid of the pain to try again.

But he had to try—had to get that shooting iron out. Because he had no doubt the farmers would ventilate him. They were out for T Bar blood.

Dusty was reconciling himself to his fate when, to his astonishment, Andy Terrill showed up.

A dyed-in-the-wool cowboy would have dabbed the loop of his lasso over Dusty's saddle horn in no time at all and pulled the dying horse up and off of Dusty's busted leg. But Andy was no hand with a lariat, and knew it. So he dismounted, reata in hand. Then his horse started acting up, disturbed by hot lead buzzing in his ears. Andy found he couldn't hold onto his cayuse with one hand and affix the loop of his rope around Dusty's saddle horn with the other. Precious seconds were wasted while he vainly struggled with this dilemma. He finally opted to let go of his horse.

"You fool!" yelled Dusty. "Now you're as dead as I am."

"We're not dead yet," replied Andy.

His next problem was dodging the flailing hooves of the dying horse. More precious seconds trickled by.

"Shoot him!" rasped Dusty. "Put a bullet in his brainpan."

Of course, thought Andy. It was the humane thing to do. He tugged the Forehand & Adams out of his belt, aimed at the animal's head, thumbed the hammer back.

"What are you waiting for?" asked Dusty through clenched teeth. "It to die of old age, for God's sake?"

Andy steeled himself to the task at hand. He had never killed anything. It was a very difficult thing for him to do. Squeezing his eyes shut, he pulled the trigger. The horse made a sharp, funny noise as the bullet struck home. Andy felt sick to his stomach. But the animal was out of its misery.

"Get that rope on the horn!" yelled Torn as he galloped up.

Andy complied. Torn put the claybank's reins between his teeth and began to fire down into the hollow as fast as he could work the repeater's action. He aimed over the heads of the oncoming homesteaders. He wasn't too sure why, but he did.

Maybe old Doc Wingate's been chewing on my conscience too much.

His efforts had the desired effect. The charge of the plow pushers lost steam. Some of them turned their mounts and headed back for the far rim. Others dismounted and commenced to answering Torn's fire with their own.

Meanwhile, Andy had succeeded in attaching the lariat to Dusty's saddle horn.

"Throw it to me," said Torn. "And get ready to pull him clear."

Andy tossed the rope. Torn dallied it around the apple of his own rig and kicked the claybank. The horse jumped, the rope sang tautly. The claybank reared and began to kettle against the deadweight anchor. Torn held on for dear life. Then the claybank settled down and seemed to comprehend what was expected of it. It pulled against the rope, lifting the carcass of Dusty's horse just enough so that Andy could drag the cowboy free.

"He's clear!" yelled Andy.

Torn drew the saber knife from its shoulder rig and slashed at the lariat, cutting it in two with one stroke. Reins once more in hand, he wheeled the claybank and drew near Andy and Dusty. On his own initiative, Andy had helped Dusty up on his one good leg, supporting Burcham by draping the cowboy's arm over his shoulder.

"Take him on behind you and go," Andy told Torn.

"What about you?" asked Dusty.

"I've got two good legs. I can run."

As Torn reached out, a bullet ripped the sleeve of his frock coat, missing his arm by a hair. He got Dusty's hand in a viselike grip and hauled up for all he was worth. Dusty sprawled across the cantle behind him. That was good enough for Torn.

"Hold on!" he shouted, kicking out of his offside stirrup. "Andy, grab hold of the stirrup."

Andy grabbed hold, and Torn pounded the claybank into a canter, but Andy almost immediately lost his grip, stumbled and sprawled. Torn swore softly and checked his horse so sharply that it almost sat down.

Jericho and the two remaining healthy T Bar cowboys arrived. While Jericho reined up near Andy, the others swept on by, yelling like wild Comanches and blasting away with their revolvers.

"Get on behind me, Mister Terrill," said Jericho, holding out a hand.

As Andy swung aboard Jericho's horse, Torn shot a look down into the hollow. The farmers had had enough. Those who hadn't beat a hasty retreat before were leaving in a hurry now. The advantage had been theirs before; now they had lost it. They weren't used to this kind of fighting.

To Torn's dismay, he saw one of the homesteaders facedown and motionless in the grass. A riderless mule was wandering off.

The two cowboys returned. One of them spoke to Torn as he reloaded his six-shooter.

"Well, it looks like I done for one."

He glanced up at Torn after the admission was made. His expression was bleak. Though he had been careful to keep his tone of voice flat and emotionless, he was clearly troubled by the knowledge that he had shot a man.

"Go check him," said Torn. "Dead or alive, put him on that mule and bring him here."

"Yes, sir," said the T Bar rider meekly. "Come on, Sam."

The two cowboys rode down into the hollow. Torn checked the far side. The farmers were long gone. All that remained was a haze of dust and gunsmoke. He didn't think they'd be coming back.

"Mister Terrill, I believe you've been plugged," remarked Jericho.

"What?"

"Well, someone's bleedin' all over my saddle, and it sure ain't me."

For the first time, Andy noticed the blood dripping from the fingers of his left hand. All trace of color drained from his face. He swayed precariously.

"Better climb down before you fall down," advised Jericho, and helped Andy dismount. Andy discovered that his knees had turned rubbery. He sat down hard in the grass. Jericho unhorsed himself and ground-hitched his pony.

"Might as well do the doctorin' here," he told Torn.

Torn nodded, and Jericho got Dusty down off the back of the claybank.

While Jericho tended to Andy, Torn saw to Dusty Burcham. He set the cowboy's broken leg and used the saddle pad off Dusty's dead horse for a makeshift splint, tying it securely with strips torn from an extra shirt he found in Dusty's war bag.

Jericho came over to inform him that Andy's wound was superficial—a bullet graze on the forearm.

"Lem's a lot worse off," said the black cowboy. "I'll go see what I can do for him." He mounted up and rode off. Fifty yards away, Lem sat slumped in the scant shade of his horse.

Torn gave Dusty a little water from his canteen. Andy was back on his feet now, and walked up. Jericho had torn the sleeve off his shirt and used it to bind his wound.

"You saved my life," said Dusty.

"I told you, I don't want anyone else getting killed over this."

"You might have been killed," replied Dusty.

"I wasn't thinking about that."

Dusty lapsed into thoughtful silence.

The two T Bar men returned with the farmer draped over the mule. Dead man's ride, thought Torn.

"He's gone under," said the rueful cowboy who had confessed to the shooting.

"My God," said Andy in despair.

Jericho was back, and looked grim. "Lem's in a bad way. Nothing I can do. Bullet's in him. We need to get him to a sawbones, quick."

"Valentine's a day's ride," said the cowboy named Sam.

"He can't make a ride like that," said Jericho.

"What do we do now, Judge?" Andy asked Torn.

"Someone needs to fetch Doc Wingate."

"I'll go," volunteered Jericho.

"Fine. The rest of you will wait here."

"Where are you going?" asked Andy.

"On to the Rosebud. I'm going to take the dead man back to his people."

"They'll gun you down for sure," said Sam.

"Maybe," said Torn. "But this is just going to get worse. I've got to try to stop it somehow."

"I'll ride with you," said Andy.

"No."

"I've got to."

"Forget it. It's too dangerous."

"I'm going," said Andy stubbornly. "They've got to see that I'm not their enemy."

Torn mulled it over. No question but that it was a dangerous proposition, riding straight into the enemy camp. If the farmers were too scared or mad or both to listen to reason, then both he and Andy Terrill were dead men. But he couldn't deny that Andy had a valid point. If a Terrill could convince them of his peaceful intentions, then just maybe . . .

"All right," said Torn.

"Just a minute," said Andy, and walked off to fetch his wayward horse.

"He's got grit," said Jericho, watching him go. "I got to admit, I sold him short first time I seen him."

"Every bit as much grit as the old man had," murmured Dusty.

Jericho looked at Dusty, surprised. The last thing he had expected to hear was an endorsement of Andy Terrill pass Dusty Burcham's lips.

When Andy returned he handed Jericho a folded piece of paper.

"What's this?" asked Gentry.

"Read it."

"I don't read too well," admitted Jericho. "In fact, not at all."

"It's a last will and testament." Andy took it back. "Come to think of it, maybe you should witness this, Judge."

Torn took the paper and read:

> I, ANDREW TERRILL, BEING OF SOUND MIND
> AND BODY, DO BEQUEATH THE T BAR RANCH
> AND ALL THE LIVESTOCK THEREON WHICH
> ARE RIGHTFULLY MY POSSESSIONS TO ALL
> THE PERSONS IN MY EMPLOY, IN EQUAL
> SHARES, AS OF THIS DATE.

Date and signature followed.

"Well I'll be," said Torn.

"What does it say?" queried Jericho.

Torn told him.

A moment of stunned silence followed. Dusty and Jericho and the other two T Bar riders were thunderstruck. They all just stared at Andy.

Andy fidgeted. "Witness that document, if you will, please, Judge," he said stiffly. "And then let's ride. As

Mister Burcham would say, we're burning daylight."
He provided Torn with a stubby charcoal pencil.

Torn signed the will and gave it to Jericho. Then he
and Andy headed east for the Rosebud, dragging the
corpse-laden mule behind them.

CHAPTER 17

DUE TO THE RECENT RAIN, THE ROSEBUD RIVER RAN HIGH and deep. Torn and Andy Terrill swam the river and decided to make camp on the other side. Darkness had fallen. There were trees here, surprisingly quite a few. Torn could have counted the trees he had seen during his sojourn in the Sand Hills on the fingers of both hands, but it was different here. He collected deadwood and built a large fire. They dried their clothes by its heat. Firelight danced in the limbs of the trees above them. Andy leaned back against his damp saddle, his hands behind his head. So engrossed was he in moody reflection on the day's events that it took him a while to realize that they were on the disputed land—enemy ground—and that Torn's fire was large enough to be seen miles away in the night.

He sat up suddenly and voiced his concerns. Torn

was on the other side of the fire, cleaning his Winchester and the Colt Peacemaker with the methodical attention to detail which a smart man gives the tools of his trade.

"I know," was all Torn said.

Andy was flabbergasted.

"I want them to know we're here," added Torn.

"So they can kill us in our sleep?" asked Andy, a little shrill.

Not, he thought, that he was going to get any sleep now.

"If we try to sneak in and surprise them," explained Torn, "they'll shoot first and talk later. I'm betting they're not the type to cut our throats while we sleep."

"You're betting our lives."

"There are risks any way we do this, Andy. I figured you knew that when you volunteered to come along."

Andy mulled that over. "I need to talk to them. I don't back down from that. I just want to make sure I get the chance."

Torn fed a few more sizable sticks of wood onto the fire. The flames leapt higher in a shower of sparks.

"You got to ask yourself," said Torn calmly, "if trying to save lives is worth risking your own."

"I believe it is."

"I could tell, earlier today, when you went back for Dusty Burcham."

"Anyone would have done the same," said Andy, embarrassed.

Torn shook his head. "Not so. But get some sleep. Don't worry about waking up alive tomorrow."

"Easy for you to say," protested Andy. "I'd like to see you do it."

He did.

Torn finished cleaning his weapons and then rolled up in his just-dried blanket, using his saddle for a pillow. He closed his eyes and went right off to sleep. Andy couldn't believe it. He watched and listened suspiciously, thinking Torn was playing possum just to prove a point. But eventually he was convinced that Torn was in fact sound asleep.

The man isn't human, thought Andy.

Or maybe he is just more man than I am.

Andy wasn't sure. Since he was wide awake anyway, with no prospect of any sleep at all that night, he lay back against his saddle and watched the firelight dance in the trees and listened like all get-out for the stealthy approach of men with harmful intent and occupied his mind with thoughts regarding Clay Torn.

He admired many of Torn's qualities. The judge was tough and tough-minded. Strong, physically as well as mentally. He shared many traits with Andy's father. Traits Andy had always felt were lacking in himself.

But in a way he felt sorry for Torn. Andy was a sensitive person—too sensitive, his father had said—and he could tell there was something tragic about Clay Torn. Something bleak and unfinished. The man was strong, but he wasn't whole. There was an emptiness in the man. A chink in the armor. Andy could see the emptiness in Torn's flint-gray eyes. Torn was a man in search of the rest of himself, an essential part that was missing. Without that part the man would never be whole. His life was meaningless. Ironically, that was a source of Torn's strength. Because he didn't think his life was worth so much that he was afraid to risk it.

Torn wasn't really afraid to die.

Which was why he could sleep while the fire drew their adversaries ever closer through the night.

Andy was sure they were coming.

He could almost feel their hate.

In spite of this, he did eventually drift off into a light sleep.

And woke, in a moment of strangling panic, to the cold caress of a gun barrel against his forehead.

"Just kill him and be done with it, Jubal," growled a voice out of the darkness. "Blow his stinking head off."

"Naw," said the man who had his shotgun planted against Andy's skull. "I got a better idea, friends. Let's hang him. Hang him high, like they hanged Matt Caldwell."

"Who's got a rope?" queried a third voice.

"He's got one on his saddle," said the man named Jubal. "We'll use it."

"Hang him with his own rope," someone said.

"Get up, you," snarled Jubal.

Andy hesitated, horrified by the mental image of his dangling by a length of hemp from one of the trees. Besides, he didn't think he *could* stand up.

"Get up!" yelled Jubal, and poked Andy in the ribs, hard.

Andy found it difficult to drag his gaze away from that menacing shotgun, but he managed, throwing a scared look around, judging his chances of escape.

There were six men standing around the camp. One bent down to add some wood to the bed of orange embers, all that remained of their campfire. The wood ignited quickly. Flames danced high, throwing more light on the subject. Andy could tell the men were farmers. And he could also tell by their expressions that they took him for a range rider. Too bad, he thought, that he had exchanged his city clothes for cowboy garb.

He stood up, shaky, and Jubal stuck the double-barreled fuke into his stomach while another man grabbed him and pinned his arms behind his back.

Belatedly, Andy remembered Torn. Panic had turned his mind to mush, but now he realized something was missing, and that something was Torn.

Where was he?

"What have you done to . . . ?"

"Shut up," snapped Jubal. "I'll ask the questions. You got a lot of gall, crossing the river alone, and Joe Turner's corpse with you."

Alone!

Andy looked wildly around again, searching for any sign of Judge Torn.

Nothing.

No sign whatsoever that Torn had ever been in the camp. Andy was confused, and then felt betrayed. Had Torn slipped away? Had he lost his nerve and run like a coward in the dark, leaving Andy to his fate? If so, Andy had surely misjudged the man. It just didn't seem like something Torn would be capable of.

But what other explanation could there be?

Another of the homesteaders stepped forward, standing shoulder to shoulder with Jubal. His expression was marginally less hostile than those of the others. He looked more perplexed, troubled, than anything.

"What are you doing here?" he asked. "Who are you?"

Andy swallowed the lump in his throat. He was suddenly afraid to tell them his name. He wondered if Jubal's shotgun would go off the instant the name Terrill passed his lips.

"I know you ride for the T Bar," said the man. "Your horse wears that brand. And it's a brand we all have reason to remember."

The others muttered angry agreement.

"I . . . I came to bring the dead man home," said Andy.

"A fool's errand," replied the man, frowning. "What kind of new Terrill trick is this?"

"No trick. We . . . I figured he had a family, and they have a right to his mortal remains. It . . . it seemed like the Christian thing to do."

Jubal snorted, derisive. "Christian! Since when did a T Bar man think like that?"

"After everything that's happened," said the other man, "weren't you worried we might get a hankering to shoot you?"

"It occurred to me."

"You're either a very brave man or a very big fool."

"Maybe they're the same."

"The dead man's name was Joe Turner. He was a friend of ours. So was Matt Caldwell. My name is Lessing. Luther Lessing. Matt Caldwell was my brother-in-law."

Andy had begun to hope he had found a reasonable man in the bunch. Now he felt that hope drain away.

"We're wasting time," complained Jubal. "Let him make his peace with God, since he's so Christian. If he can. Then we'll string him up and be done with it."

"You're quick to take another man's life, Jubal," said Lessing, with mild reproof.

"No quicker than these T Bar men. He probably killed Turner himself."

"No," said Andy.

"We're at war, Luther," pressed Jubal. "No use trying to deny it. And men die in war. The other day we all agreed we weren't going to let them run us out. We agreed to stand and fight for what was ours by right. You were there. You threw in with the rest of us. You shouldn't have done, if you weren't ready to do some killing."

"I'm never *ready* to kill," replied Lessing sternly. "But I will if I have to. I did plenty of killing in the war. Too much. When it was over I swore I'd never fire a gun in anger again. Still, I'll do what I have to to protect my home and my family. I'm just not sure that includes hanging this man. He's hardly more than a boy, really."

"He wouldn't think twice about gunning you down," declared Jubal.

"That's not true!" protested Andy. "How can you say that? You don't know me. That's the whole problem here."

"I don't know you, and I don't want to," said Jubal. "But I know your kind. And they make me sick. Looking down on us like we're dirt."

"I don't do that," said Andy. "I'm trying to tell you . . ."

"Save it," growled Jubal. "A man who's about to die will say anything."

"In war," said Lessing, "after the battle was over, both sides would abide by an unspoken truce, so that they could collect their dead. The boy didn't come to do more killing. He came to bring Joe's body back."

"I say hang him," said Jubal. "Or he might be killing us tomorrow."

Lessing looked around, trying to read the faces of the other farmers. Andy did likewise. He didn't like what he saw by the hellish light of the campfire.

"I say we don't hang him," said Lessing. "Who agrees with me?"

No one spoke.

Lessing shook his head. He looked down at his boots a moment, then met Andy's gaze.

"I'm sorry, boy. It's five to one for hanging you."

"Five to two," said Torn.

The farmers whirled to see the man in black step out of night shadows into the throw of firelight.

"And I've got six .45-caliber friends with me," added Torn, wagging the Colt Peacemaker. "They'll speak against a lynching, too. So I guess that tips the scales."

CHAPTER

18

JUBAL WAS THE ONLY ONE AMONG THE FARMERS WHO thought about lead-slinging. A hundred times before, Torn had walked into a situation like this, and he knew how to read his adversaries. The eyes gave them away. Expressions could be deceiving. Some men could smile and the next second gun you down. Others could look convincingly belligerent and mask the fear gnawing away at their insides. But the eyes never lied. They telegraphed the action the person was about to take. And Torn could see in Jubal's eyes that the farmer's shotgun was about to speak death.

So he fired the Colt Peacemaker.

He didn't give warning. Didn't try to talk Jubal out of it.

A man could get killed, talking when he should be shooting.

The bullet smashed into Jubal's right shoulder and spun him around. He dropped the shotgun, clutched his right arm, which had gone completely numb, and fell to his knees.

Lessing made a move to retrieve the shotgun. Torn's Colt swung his way.

"There's been enough killing," said Torn.

Lessing looked at Jubal, then back at Torn.

"What kind of shot are you?"

Torn smiled. "Good enough. I could have killed him. I'm glad to see there's one among you who keeps his wits about him."

Lessing nodded and slowly stepped away from the shotgun.

"All of you, drop your weapons. And let him go." This last command was directed at the man who held Andy.

The farmers exchanged grim looks. Torn knew what they were thinking—that the odds were still five to one in their favor, and they could probably get him. But at what cost? The bottom line was this: none of them wanted to be the next Jubal.

In the end, they chose to comply. Released, Andy just stood there, dumbfounded, staring at Torn. Comprehension was a slow dawning in his eyes.

"You set me up," he breathed. "You used me as bait."

"Stand clear, Andy."

"I could have been killed."

"I had you covered the whole time."

Shaking like a leaf, Andy pointed at Jubal. "He might have just walked up and blown my head off. No way you could know for sure."

"I told you it was a risky business. Now stop belly-aching. Might-have-beens are as worthless as a three-legged horse. You're still alive. Settle for that."

"So it was a trick," said Lessing bitterly.

"No," said Torn. "He told you the truth, for the most part. And he didn't know what I was doing. He almost gave me away. But we didn't come for trouble. We came to talk."

"It's late for talk," said Lessing. "You don't think we would have preferred talking it out, at the beginning? But Lane Terrill wouldn't listen. Now good men lie dead."

"It's never too late," insisted Torn. "Andy, tell them who you are."

"I'm Lane Terrill's son."

"Well I'll be damned," said Lessing, astonished.

Andy drew himself up, made an effort to stop shaking. "My father's dead. You're dealing with me now."

"Matt Caldwell didn't kill your father."

"How do you know?" asked Torn.

"Because his wife is my sister, and they were over to my place that night Lane Terrill got bushwhacked. Of course, I don't expect you to believe that. But it's true. Nobody bothered to ask me when those T Bar men dragged Matt out of his bed and lynched him."

"And you were about to do the same thing to me," said Andy, without rancor. He was just trying to make a point.

Lessing nodded. "I see what you're trying to say."

"And I believe you," added Andy. "About Caldwell."

"So do I," said Torn. He could tell Lessing was a man of integrity. A man of reason. One who could be trusted to tell the truth. Torn felt for the first time some real hope that this tragic misunderstanding between the farmers and the T Bar could be settled.

"Who are you, anyway?" Lessing asked him.

"Clay Torn. Federal judge."

"The one they sent to settle the land dispute."

"I have," said Torn.

"Just like that? You don't want to hear our side of it?"

"I know your side of it."

"You can keep the land," said Andy. "It's not worth men's lives."

"It is if you don't have any to call your own."

"Well, you do now."

"My God. We almost hanged you."

Andy walked up to Lessing and stuck out his hand.

"You'll have no more trouble with the T Bar. You've got my word on that."

For a moment, Lessing looked at the proffered hand.

Then he shook it.

"I feel I can trust you." He turned to Torn. "But what about the men who killed Caldwell?"

"What do you want done?"

Lessing shook his head, glanced at the other farmers. They seemed content to let him speak for them.

"I've got killers on my payroll," said Andy. "But I don't know if I'll ever find out who they are unless they step forward and confess. Still, they're not bad men, Mister Lessing. Not really. They acted out of anger and grief."

"Just like we acted here tonight. I'm inclined to let it go. It happened. Matt's gone. More bloodshed won't bring it back."

"Those men will have to live with what they've done for the rest of their lives," said Andy, grim. "I wouldn't want that on my conscience. And I wouldn't want to have to answer for it on Judgment Day."

"Which leaves us with one question," said Torn.

"Who killed Lane Terrill?" said Lessing.

Torn's slate-gray eyes raked across the faces of the other farmers. "Might not have been Caldwell. But it could have been one of you."

One said "No" flat out. Two shook their heads. The others stared.

"Or all this might have been a scheme to kill Lane Terrill from the very start."

"What?" exclaimed Andy.

"A scheme by somebody who wanted your father dead. Who saw the perfect opportunity when the Rosebud River changed its course. Because he knew what Lane Terrill would do. Start a war. And in war, people get killed."

"Quarles?" asked Andy. "You mean Joshua Quarles?"

"He's a suspect, certainly. If I'm right, it was a brilliant plan. Putting the farmers on the disputed land, so that when your father was murdered everyone would naturally assume one of them did it."

"Joshua Quarles is a decent man," said Lessing. "I can't believe that."

"Because he sold you this land for next to nothing?" responded Andy. "He was using you. At the very least he didn't want to get into a shooting match with the T Bar. And maybe he did it for another reason, if what Judge Torn says is true."

"So what happens now?" asked Lessing.

"Bury the hatchet between the two of you," Torn told Lessing and Andy. "And bury your dead. Then you hang up your guns and try to live as good neighbors from now on."

"That'll work for me," said Lessing.

The other farmers nodded and murmured agreement.

Lessing gave Andy a long look, then turned to the rest of the homesteaders. "A couple of you give Jubal a hand and let's go home."

They picked up their guns. Two of them helped their gunshot friend, while a third collected the mule bearing the body of Joe Turner. In a show of good faith, Torn holstered his Colt. He thought it a safe bet that the farmers were finished with fighting. He and Andy watched them disappear into the darkness.

"If Quarles killed my father," said Andy, "you'll have the devil's own time proving it."

"I don't think he pulled the trigger."

"Then who?"

"Olin Treadway has a bunch of hired killers on his payroll. I'd bet my last dollar one of them was the man who back shot your father."

"Olin Treadway," muttered Andy, frowning. "Why do I feel as though I know that name? Who is he?"

"Runs a saloon in Valentine. Well, actually, he runs most of Keno Street."

"Is there some connection between Quarles and Treadway?"

"I'll let you know when I find out."

"I want to help."

"No. You run your ranch, Andy. Leave justice to me." Torn checked the eastern sky. "False dawn.

Since they were kind enough to build the fire back up for us, we might as well brew some java."

An hour later they parted company. Andy headed back for the T Bar, while Torn pointed the claybank in the direction of Valentine.

CHAPTER

19

WHEN HE GOT BACK TO TOWN TORN HANDED THE CLAYBANK over to Kostmyer and made his way to the Plainsman. The desk clerk put down his dime novel long enough to provide him with paper, pen, and ink. Torn spent most of the afternoon in his room writing. He took the finished product to the office of the town newspaper, the Valentine *Courier*.

The *Courier's* editor was a small, tousled, older man with a shock of unkempt white hair. His name was George Battenfield. He chewed vigorously on an unlit stogie while reading what Torn had written, his feet propped up on a cluttered rolltop desk. Torn tried to mask his impatience by studying the Washington two-pull printing press which took up most of the office space.

"Not bad," said Battenfield finally. "Not very eloquent. Sparse. But to the point. You've had a good education."

"University of Virginia."

"Indeed. When?"

"It was another lifetime."

"I was looking forward to covering the hearing which I assumed you would call to hear both sides of the dispute."

"I've already made a decision. There it is in black and white."

"And you want me to print it."

Torn nodded. "Today."

"This last part. Pure conjecture?"

"Matt Caldwell didn't kill Lane Terrill."

"And you intend to remain in Valentine and investigate Terrill's murder."

"Right."

"Sounds suspiciously like you are throwing down the gauntlet."

"I am. And the man who picks it up is the one I'm after."

Battenfield took a deep breath, stood up, and came forward to shake Torn's hand. His grip was surprisingly strong for one so old and advanced in years.

"I'd heard some bad things about you, Judge. How you picked a fight in the Bull's-eye Saloon. How you bullied Sheriff Mackey, God rest his soul. I was all set to write a scathing editorial for next Saturday's edition, excoriating the federal judicial system for employing men such as you."

"Excoriating?" Torn smiled.

"Harvard."

"Can't wait to read that editorial."

"You never will. I don't know how you did it, but you brought peace to the banks of the Rosebud."

"Now that's eloquent."

"Words are more powerful than bullets, in the long run."

"So you'll get this out today."

"Special edition. It will hit the streets before dark."

"I want to make sure Joshua Quarles and Olin Treadway get a copy."

"There's a young man by the name of Billy Oates who runs messages out of town for the telegraph office . . ."

"Yes, the Paul Revere of Cherry County."

Battenfield chuckled. "I'll send a copy out to the Quarles ranch by him. And I'll have a whole stack of them delivered to the Bull's-eye Saloon." He looked sidelong at Torn. "What are you trying to achieve, Judge?"

"Just trying to smoke the rats out of the woodwork, Mister Battenfield."

"The man who killed Lane Terrill."

"And the man who hired him to do it."

He returned to the hotel. Having gotten precious little sleep last night waiting for the farmers to stumble into his trap, he was exhausted. Yet sleep eluded him. Thoughts of Rose Pendergast kept him awake and restless. He wanted to be with her. Even though it wasn't fair to either of them. There was the pain of parting to be weighed against the pain of being apart. Life, he thought, gave you no easy answers.

Wrestling with his conscience until dinnertime, he postponed the decision for a walk to the Blue Chip Restaurant. Battenfield's one-page special edition of the *Courier* was just out. Torn smiled at the big banner headline. PEACE ON THE ROSEBUD! In slightly smaller print below this: JUDGE TORN SEEKS LANE TERRILL'S KILLER. Battenfield had penned a very eloquent and fiery editorial excoriating those who took the law into their own hands, and urged the T Bar riders who were responsible for the death of the innocent Matt Caldwell to give themselves up.

Torn dawdled over his food. Finally, disgusted with himself for being so indecisive, he threw his napkin on the table and stalked out of the restaurant, scowling.

Night had fallen. The Yellow Rose was ablaze with light. A half-dozen horses stood along the tie rails. The Oriental girl answered the door.

"I've come to . . ." began Torn.

"Yes. Come in please."

The doors to the parlor to the left of the hall were open. A man wearing sleeve garters and a bowler hat set at a jaunty angle was playing the piano, and several women in bright silk and satin were making their cowboy clients comfortable. The Oriental girl ushered him into the parlor across the hall. Torn paced nervously. The minutes turned to hours. He rehearsed what he was going to say, over and over again. But when Rose came in he forgot everything.

"Clay."

"Hello, Rose."

Neither spoke for a moment. Torn shifted from one foot to the other. The ghost of a smile touched her lips.

"Rose, I . . . hell."

She let him off the hook, going to him, putting her arms around his neck and brushing his lips with hers. He grabbed her and pulled her close, holding on for dear life, and felt her tears on his face.

* * *

He slept in a warm cocoon of a feather bed, cool sheets, and Rose Pendergast's velvet skin. They made love and he refused to think about the consequences —about tomorrow. That was difficult for him to do. For so many years he had been living in the past and for the future. On the best of days he woke with the hope that before the sun set he would find Melony Hancock and life could begin again. On the worst of days, when he awoke full of despair, he let the ghosts of the past haunt him, the "might-have-beens," and the resulting guilt drove him on.

He slept well, better than he had in a long time. But the instincts, honed to perfection by a life of violence, never slept, and when the discreet tapping came, he snapped instantly awake and reached without conscious thought for the Colt in the holster on the bedside table.

Rose placed a hand on his arm.

"It's only Lotus, Clay."

Early morning light leaked into the room around the edges of the green shades on the tall windows, and touched her tousled golden hair, and he stared, marveling at how beautiful she was—still, after such a hard life—and then he looked quickly away, realizing what danger lurked in staring too long and thinking such thoughts.

But then she rose, and he couldn't help but look again, admiring her slender, girlish figure and the flawless alabaster skin. She put on the wrapper adorned with the rampant Chinese dragon and crossed the airy, high-ceiling room from the big canopy bed to the door.

As she and Lotus spoke in undertones which did

not reach him, he lay back, letting his head sink down into the sinfully seductive comfort of a goosedown pillow. The doubts assailed him, and with resignation he let them in. It was morning. It was tomorrow. He gauged their chances—his and Rose's—of a future together. He could do it. He could love her. That much he knew. She would be his, without reservations. But it wouldn't be complete. Because he still loved Melony. Always would. *He* had the reservations. And so he could not give himself completely to Rose.

She would accept that. At least at first. Maybe even for the duration. She was that kind of a woman. But could he accept it? The feeling that he was betraying Melony, wherever she was, if he gave up the search and selfishly settled for his own happiness. He did not fully comprehend what drove him to this obsession, because he knew Melony might be dead, or happy herself without a thought of him, but he understood the power of that obsession, and had learned to live with it. And, oftentimes, hate it. But one thing he could never do was ignore it, or dispense with it. It was there, and it stood as a wall between him and Rose, and it wasn't fair to her.

But then, neither was this.

Torn sighed. It always ended this way. Doubts and difficult decisions, when you pondered the imponderables of tomorrow, failing to live just for today.

Lotus left, the door closed, and Rose came back to bed. She crawled in on top of him, and the wrapper came undone, and the soft heat of her splendid body stirred the embers of desire inside him. Her kiss was promise and passion.

"Is something wrong?" he asked.

It broke the spell, of course, as he knew it would.

The moment was smashed to pieces like a ship hurled by an angry sea against the rocks.

"A little trouble downstairs. One of our customers. Also, one of Treadway's men."

"Who?"

"A man named Farnum. He comes here a lot. Fancies a girl named Annie. Don't worry. Rayford can handle it."

"Rayford?"

"My bartender. Also my bouncer. Now shut up and kiss me."

He did.

Gunshot.

CHAPTER

20

"STAY HERE," SNAPPED TORN. HE WAS UP AND IN HIS trousers and buckling on the gun belt before Rose even had time to figure out what was happening.

"This is my place," she said.

"Let me handle it." He grabbed the shoulder rig holding his saber knife and headed for the door, not taking the time to concern himself with boots or shirt.

"Clay . . ."

But he was gone, out of the room, down the hall and the staircase; halfway down the latter, with the saber knife's harness draped over one shoulder, he slowed down and drew the Colt Peacemaker.

The Oriental girl, Lotus, was cowering in a corner of the downstairs hall. She looked up at Torn with frightened eyes and began to move toward him. He gestured sharply for her to stay put and then placed a forefinger to his lips, indicating that he wanted her to remain silent as well.

He descended a few more steps, crouching slightly, trying to peer through the open doors to the parlor where last night he had seen the girls of the Yellow Rose entertaining their clients. At first he couldn't see anything—the angle was too great and most of the parlor remained hidden from him. Then a bottle crashed, as sudden and unnerving as a gunshot. Torn smoothed out his nerves and took a few more steps.

"I told you I wanted a drink." A gruff voice, a little slurred, from the parlor.

"And I told you the bar's closed."

The second voice was wracked with pain.

"Oh, you're a tough one," jeered the first man. "Maybe I should've just shot you dead."

"Maybe you better."

An ugly laugh. "And maybe you just don't know who you're backtalkin', barkeep."

"I know who you are, Farnum. And what you are."

Another bottle smashed.

"To hell with you," slurred Farnum.

Torn was nearly to the bottom of the stairs when a man appeared, staggering drunkenly through the parlor doorway.

He was wearing a yellow duster over range clothes.

Just like the men who had dry gulched Andy Terrill on the road from Cody.

Farnum looked at Torn. It was a moment frozen in time.

Then everything happened at once. Lotus moved, running for the stairs. Farnum had a bottle of whiskey in one hand and his six-gun in the other. He dropped the bottle and raised the gun. Torn had his Colt up and aimed and as he thumbed the hammer back he yelled "Don't try it!" because in the back of his mind he knew Farnum was worth more to him alive than dead. But in her flight Lotus crossed the line of fire, and Farnum read Torn and immediately knew that Torn wasn't going to risk shooting around her. With a twisted grin he lurched forward and grabbed her, hooking an arm around her waist and pulling her roughly to him. He backstepped toward the front door. Lotus kicked and scratched, to no avail. He picked her up bodily and used her as a human shield.

"Drop the gun, mister," sneered Farnum.

Torn knew Farnum would shoot him whether he dropped the Colt or not.

"Go to hell," he said.

"After you," said Farnum.

Torn vaulted over the staircase bannister. Farnum's six-shooter boomed. The bullet smashed the polished mahogany of the railing just as Torn cleared it. Torn hit the hallway floor and rolled. Again Farnum fired, still backing up, but Lotus's struggles disrupted his aim, and this time the bullet scarred the floor. Torn was still rolling. Nearly to the door, Farnum shoved Lotus forward, half turned for the door, and then for some reason turned back and fired twice more, wildly.

Lotus cried out and fell, shot in the back.

Torn finally got off his first shot. Too late. Farnum was out the door and running. Torn's bullet smashed the glass set into the door. He stared at the blood on Lotus's *cheongsam,* heard Farnum's boots pounding the floor planks of the veranda fronting the Yellow Rose.

A cold rage welled up inside him.

Up and running, he dashed into the parlor where he

and Rose had met for the first time upon his arrival in Valentine. Two of the parlor's windows faced the veranda. The shades were up to admit the morning's light, and Torn saw a flash of yellow duster in the first as he entered the room. No chance for the shot. Farnum was heading for the corner of the house. Torn dashed across the parlor and dived headlong through the second window. It was perfectly timed. He brought his arms up over his face and tucked his chin to protect himself from broken glass. Farnum collided with him. They both went down, but in different directions.

Farnum caromed off and fell sideways, into the veranda railing. The railing gave way and Farnum landed heavily in the street. Torn landed on the veranda in an awkward position, striking his gun arm painfully and losing his grip on the Colt. The Peacemaker skittered across the weathered planks and disappeared over the edge. Farnum, too, had lost his gun. He got up and turned for the horse at the tie rail. Torn picked himself up and leaped, landing on Farnum's back, dragging the man to the ground.

Cursing, Farnum kicked, and the heel of his boot caught Torn in the shoulder, causing such excruciating pain that for a moment Torn thought his collarbone had been broken. He lost his grip on Farnum, and Farnum wriggled loose, bounced up, and lunged for the horse again. He wasn't going for the saddle, but rather for the "hot roll" tied on behind the cantle. Reaching into the rolled blankets, he drew out a sawed-off shotgun. Torn hit him again, driving with his legs and striking low, putting his undamaged shoulder into Farnum's gut before Farnum could bring the greener to bear. Farnum landed on his back in the middle of Keno Street and Torn fell on top of him. Torn wrenched the shotgun out of his grasp and hurled it away.

"You bastard!" he said, teeth clenched, rage shaking him to the core.

He hammered a rock-hard fist into Farnum's face. Then another. And another. He heard Farnum's jaw crack with deep satisfaction. Blood sprayed his chest and face, flung out of Farnum's ruined mouth with every blow. Torn was a coldly methodical machine of destruction. The saber knife's shoulder rig was still over his shoulder. He drew the knife, and for one terrible instant was prepared to drive the blade into Farnum's heart. He could scarcely resist the urge. Farnum was completely helpless, no longer putting up resistance, just sprawled there bloody and barely conscious.

And that was what saved him.

Torn couldn't kill a defenseless man—no matter what kind of man he was. It was one of the few rules he lived by, and now it cut through the blind rage and took hold of him and shook him savagely back to sanity.

Straddling Farnum, the saber knife raised, Torn took a deep breath and blinked sweat out of his eyes. Like someone emerging from a coma, he slowly became aware of his surroundings. The gunshots had shattered the stillness of the morning, and Valentine was coming to see what had happened on Keno Street. People were at the windows and in the doorways, running out of alleys and along the boardwalks.

Farnum was fighting his way back to consciousness. He began to struggle. Torn grabbed him by the throat with his left hand and squeezed.

"Who killed Lane Terrill?"

Farnum made incoherent noises. Torn could tell by their pitch and Farnum's truculent expression that whatever the man was trying to say, it wasn't nice. He flailed at Torn with his fists.

Torn drove the saber knife to the hilt in Farnum's leg.

The man's guttural scream sent a shudder down Torn's spine.

"Tell me who killed Lane Terrill," hissed Torn.

Still Farnum fought. Torn steeled himself, then twisted the blade. The act horrified him. He almost lost his resolve. He was a violent man, but not a brutal one, and this went against the grain. But there was no more time. He was at a crossroads, without alternatives. What could he do? Put Farnum in jail? Treadway would get him out. Farnum would disappear, as Booth and Grizzly had disappeared. Or Treadway would have Farnum killed, as he had done Sheriff Mackey. Torn knew he was playing a desperate game against desperate foes. There were no rules, not for the winner. Even so, only the fact that Farnum had killed Lotus gave Torn the wherewithal to do what he was doing—the most brutal thing he had ever done.

Farnum's body arched off the ground, and the man's howl of agony seemed to freeze everyone in the street in their tracks. Torn held Farnum down and kept a firm grip on the saber knife.

"Who killed Lane Terrill?"

"I did!" screamed Farnum. *"I did, damn you!"*

"Treadway paid you."

Farnum nodded.

"Say it."

"Treadway," gasped Farnum. His eyes were beginning to glaze; he was beginning that long slide into unconsciousness. "Treadway . . . told me . . . do it . . ."

He passed out.

Torn looked up. Doc Wingate was standing a dozen feet away, medical grip in hand. He was staring at Torn as he might have stared at some hideous creature who had just arisen from the bowels of Hell. Completely drained, Torn got to his feet. He left the saber knife in Farnum's leg.

"Got some more work for you, Doc," said Torn bitterly, and turned away.

Back inside the Yellow Rose, he found Rose Pendergast kneeling beside the body of the Oriental girl. Rose had Lotus's hand cupped in her hands.

"She's gone," said Rose flatly. She wasn't crying.

Torn nodded wearily and walked on by to climb the stairs.

CHAPTER 21

TORN SPENT THE MORNING IN THE SHERIFF'S OFFICE.

He sent for Kostmyer, and the livery owner provided a stout chain and padlock for the purpose of securing the door to Farnum's cell. Somebody else still had the key to the jail, and Torn figured it was Olin Treadway. When Kostmyer gave him the key to the padlock, Torn dropped it down inside his boot.

Doc Wingate came next, ostensibly to check on his patient. Farnum had lost a lot of blood from the knife wound in his thigh, even though the blade had missed the main artery, and the cracked jaw was giving him a lot of pain. More than he could handle. Wingate administered another dose of laudanum.

Torn sat behind the desk in the sheriff's office, feet propped up, sharpening the blade of the saber knife on a whetstone. Wingate came to stand across the desk from him, and one glance at the doctor's face told Torn what was coming.

"I don't want to hear it," he said, and went back to work on the saber knife.

But Wingate would not be denied.

"It's starting all over again. Just like Lincoln."

Torn said nothing.

"Innocent people caught in the cross fire. Lotus was the first. How many more, Judge?"

"Time enough for the body count when the shooting's finished."

Wingate shook his head. "You're not that cold-blooded. You can't be. There's got to be some compassion inside you. Some mercy. Simple humanity."

"Just trying to live up to your expectations."

"When I read the special edition yesterday, I thought I had misjudged you. You did the right thing, siding with the farmers regarding the disputed land. And I was surprised to hear that peace had been struck between the T Bar and the homesteaders."

"All it took was a couple of reasonable men."

"But then I saw you put that . . . that knife in Farnum's leg. I saw you twist it. It was the most . . . the most savage act I have ever witnessed."

Torn nodded. "Yes. I'll have to live with it. I had a good teacher. A man named Schmidt. He was a federal sergeant, posted to the prisoner-of-war camp at Point Lookout, which is where I spent the last year and a half of the war. It became his mission in life to break me. He knew how to inflict pain. He enjoyed it."

"Is that an excuse for what you did today?"

"No excuses. But I got what I wanted. Lane Terrill's killer."

"The end justifies the means?"

"I don't know."

"Farnum killed Terrill?"

"And Treadway put him up to it."

"So what are you waiting for? Why don't you go kill Treadway now?"

"You wouldn't believe me if I told you."

"Try me."

Torn wiped the blade of the saber knife clean on his pants leg and secured it in the shoulder harness beneath his black frock coat.

"Because I'm hoping he'll run, Doc. He'll either run or come for me. If he runs, I'll go after him. I'd prefer it that way, because then we won't have to turn Valentine into a battlefield."

Wingate was silent a moment, pondering these words.

"You really mean that," he decided.

Torn grimaced, got up and walked over to the potbelly stove in the corner to pour himself a cup of java from an enamel coffeepot.

"I don't know about you, Torn. I guess it's true what they say—that there's good and bad in every person. But in you, good and bad are waging one hell of a war, and I'd say so far it's a draw."

Turning sharply, Torn laid the daguerreotype of Melony Hancock on the desk.

"There's the good in me, Doc. I lost it twelve years ago. It was my fault for losing it. I rode off to fight and took for granted she would be there when I got back. But she wasn't. And so I've got to find her. And I have to keep looking, even if it takes me until Judgment Day."

Wingate looked at the daguerreotype for a long time. Then he nodded slowly.

"I'll pray you find her. For your sake, I hope you do, and soon. Because you're walking on the edge. One wrong step and you're just as bad as the men you're fighting. Just as bad as that man Schmidt."

"I know. He had a hand in making me what I am today. And I've walked that edge for years. God knows, I'm tired of it."

Shortly after Wingate took his leave, Rose arrived. She was accompanied by the Oriental man Torn remembered seeing at the hash counter in the Bull's-eye Saloon.

"This is Soong Lee," said Rose. "He works for Olin Treadway."

"I know."

"He was also Lotus's lover."

Soong Lee was distraught. His face was twisted with inconsolable grief. His eyes were swollen from crying. Torn could commiserate. He knew what it felt like to lose the one you loved.

"We were to be married," said Soong Lee in passable English.

"Did Treadway know this?"

Soong Lee shook his head. "We tell no one. We afraid, because . . ." He glanced at Rose.

"Because of the problem between Treadway and me," said Rose. "But Lotus confided in me some time ago. She and I have . . . had no secrets." Her voice quavered, and she struggled to maintain her composure.

"Well," said Torn, "I'm truly sorry, Soong Lee. I know that doesn't help a whole hell of a lot."

"It not your fault."

"I feel it is, partly."

"Treadway's fault. Farnum kill Lotus, and he work for Treadway. Treadway to blame." Soong Lee had made up his mind. Torn figured it had to be so, for Soong Lee to rationalize what he was about to do.

The man had come to betray Olin Treadway. Torn could feel it in his bones. He was about to get the answers he needed.

"So what do you know about what's been happening?" he asked.

"Soong Lee know plenty. I watch. I listen. They do not see me. They call me dumb Chinaman. But I not dumb. I know."

"Tell me what you know."

"I with Treadway long time. Years ago, Treadway beat T Bar cowboy with these." Soong Lee held up clenched fists. "Cowboy look too much at woman who work with Treadway. She was a gambler. Cheat cowboys at cards. She was Treadway's woman. The cowboy, he die later. He work for Lane Terrill. Terrill ride into town with his men. They burn Treadway's place. Terrill beat Treadway, like Treadway beat Terrill's man. Only Treadway lives. Takes a long time to get well. But never get well inside. Full of hate for Lane Terrill."

Torn glanced at Rose. She said, "This happened before I came to Valentine. But I've heard about it. It happened that way."

"What happened to the woman?" Torn asked Soong Lee.

"She go away. But Treadway would not run away."

"And he waited this long for vengeance."

"He was afraid of Terrill, don't you see?" asked Rose. "Which is why he hired all those gunslingers."

"From what I've heard of Lane Terrill, I'm surprised he didn't run Treadway out of Valentine."

"Lane didn't have to run Treadway out of town just so he could sleep at night. He figured he'd taught Treadway a lesson. I guess he underestimated the man. Treadway had it in for Lane from then on. He just sat back and waited for his chance."

"At first he say he will own all of Keno Street," said Soong Lee. "That way, no T Bar cowboy get a fair shake when he come to Valentine for good time."

"But he finally did tell Farnum to kill Terrill," said Torn.

"That may have been because of me," admitted Rose.

"You? Well, you told me Treadway wanted you for himself, but what does . . . ?"

"So did Lane Terrill, Clay. He was a very lonely man after his wife left him. I guess I should have told you, but . . ."

Torn smiled. "I'm not surprised, Rose. It just proves that Lane Terrill had good taste."

"I didn't love him."

"You don't have to explain."

"I will if I want to," said Rose crossly. "I didn't love him. But I . . . I was afraid of Treadway. And I knew Treadway was afraid of Lane. So I . . ." She faltered.

"We do what we have to," said Torn, without reproach.

"Like everyone else, I assumed Caldwell killed Lane. Now I know different. Now I know it was about me. I used Lane to protect me from Treadway. I let him think there was a chance for us. I was nice to him. I used him, and he was murdered because of me."

"Did you actually hear Treadway tell Farnum to kill Lane Terrill?" Torn asked Soong Lee.

"I hear."

"Will you testify to that, if need be?"

Soong Lee glanced at the cell occupied by Farnum. The gun slick was motionless on his bunk. Torn thought he was asleep. The laudanum had taken effect by now, diminishing the pain. Soong Lee was clearly fearful of Farnum—of all the hired killers on Treadway's payroll. But he wanted revenge, needed it, and that need overruled his fear.

He nodded. "I will."

"Is Treadway at the Bull's-eye?"

"No. He leave town."

"How long ago."

Soong Lee shrugged. "One hour. Maybe less."

"And that's when you came to Rose."

Again Soong Lee nodded.

"He took The Cimarron Kid with him, Clay," said Rose.

"Then I'd better get on their trail."

"I know where they go," said Soong Lee. "Old line shack on Quarles Ranch."

"So Quarles is involved."

"I don't think so," said Rose. "I don't think he knows."

"If not, I guess I owe him an apology."

"Be careful, Clay. Soong Lee says the line shack is where Booth and Grizzly and one other hired gun are hiding out."

"Good. Soong Lee, can you tell me how to find this place?"

Soong Lee told him. Torn grabbed his Winchester 44/40 and headed for the door.

"Clay."

He turned back to her.

"Clay, will you come back?"

He touched her cheek. "Don't worry, Rose. I'll come back."

But he could not look her in the eye as he said it.

CHAPTER 22

TORN CROSSED THE NIOBRARA ON THE FERRY AND TURNED east, following the river. He could look up the long slope of grass and see Two Mile Pine, beneath which Lane Terrill lay buried, and he touched the brim of his hat, a gesture of respect.

He was going after the man responsible for putting Terrill in his grave, going with his guns loaded and his saber knife sharpened. It would end in a way Terrill would understand—the only way Terrill knew—in a blaze of gunfire, a baptism of blood. Treadway and his hired hellions wouldn't give up without a fight. That much was certain. Torn figured that would suit Lane Terrill just fine.

He thought about Terrill and Rose Pendergast. He was sorry for Rose that Lane was dead. Maybe it would have worked out between the two of them. He wasn't sure what kind of man Terrill had been—what kind of husband he would have been for Rose. Hard to say. Just a man, with both good and bad in him, like Doc Wingate had said. But Torn had a hunch that Terrill had been the last best hope for Rose.

Poor Rose. She felt guilty for using Terrill. Claimed she hadn't loved him—had merely used him to shield herself from Olin Treadway's unwelcome attentions. On the face of it, not a very proper motive for getting married. The poets said you needed love for that. Torn wasn't sure if that was necessarily so. At least Rose would have had someone. Terrill had probably really loved her. She was easy to love.

He rode on beneath the blistering afternoon sun, across a sea of grass, unconcerned about what might lay ahead. Too many times he had ridden into battle. During the first months of the War Between the States, in his youth and inexperience, he had fretted over the future—and if he even had one—on the eve of a battle. He had learned that worrying didn't do anything but cost a man his sleep. What happened, happened. Worrying never changed anything.

So instead of worrying, Torn tried to put himself in Treadway's shoes. Why had the man chosen flight over taking the fight to Torn? Clearly he was seeking shelter behind his gang of hired guns. Because he knew Torn would be coming for him.

At first glance, and by his reputation, Treadway gave the impression of a man who would not even think of running from a fight. He was supposed to be a terror with his bare fists. A dangerous man, Rose had said. A man who had beaten a cowboy to death. But in reality, Treadway was nothing more than a bully. Every bully had a yellow streak. They only fought when they knew they couldn't lose. In this way, Treadway was much like Karl Schmidt. He didn't mind throwing his weight around when he had the upper hand. But when the odds were even, well, that was a horse of an entirely different color. Schmidt, like all cowards, had died poorly. He had wept and pleaded for his life. Torn had shown him no mercy. And he would show none to Treadway. The man had caused too much misery. He was responsible for too much death.

It did not surprise Torn, now that he knew the truth, that Treadway had sent his hirelings to waylay Andy Terrill on the road from Cody. Treadway had signed Andy's death warrant for no other reason than that Andy was Lane Terrill's flesh and blood. There had never been any connection between the dry gulching of Andy Terrill and the dispute between the homesteaders and the T Bar Ranch. Treadway's hatred for Lane Terrill had simply run so deep in his dark soul that he had wanted to destroy his enemy's son out of sheer, malevolent spite.

No, thought Torn. No mercy for this man.

If there was both good and bad in Olin Treadway, in Torn's judgment the good was so scant it wasn't worth saving.

By the things he had done, Treadway had signed his own death warrant.

And Torn was willing to carry out the execution.

The day drew to a close. Darkness descended upon the Sand Hills. Still Torn rode on. A cooling night wind whispered in the tall grass. Coyotes sang to the early moon. The claybank was a "long" horse, with plenty of bottom, and kept on tirelessly.

Several hours into the night, Torn rode to the rim of

a horseshoe-shaped ridge and finally stopped. Two hundred yards along the rim was a sod house. By Soong Lee's description, Torn knew this to be the abandoned Quarles Ranch line shack Treadway's gun slicks used as a hideout.

Lamplight burned yellow in the windows. A gray wisp of smoke from a cow chip fire leaked out of the chimney. In the moonlight, Torn could see every detail with remarkable clarity. To his left, at the foot of the ridge, the Niobrara was a silver snake twisting through the hills.

Torn dismounted, ground-hitching the claybank, and drawing the Winchester 44/40 from its saddle boot. Beyond the sod house was a rope corral, and in this stood a bunch of horses. Testing the wind, Torn found it to be blowing from the south, from his right to his left. He was not downwind of the horses; they would not pick up his scent, or that of the claybank.

He studied the sod house for quite some time, looking for a sentry, expecting there to be one. But he could see nothing to indicate the presence of a lookout. This perplexed him. It didn't make any sense, if Treadway was worried about him.

Never one to shy away from taking chances, Torn moved closer, walking upright but stepping cautiously, making no sudden moves, as alert and stealthy as a wolf stalking its prey.

He closed to within a hundred yards of the sod house before dropping to one knee in the grass. Watching the corral for several minutes, he finally concluded there were five horses. All were saddled, ready for the quick getaway.

Torn switched his attention back to the sod house as the front door swung open, spilling a rectangle of yellow light on the ground. A man emerged, and by his size Torn knew immediately it was Grizzly. Grizzly lumbered around the corner of the house out of sight. He returned a moment later, adjusting his trousers, and went back inside.

For a while, Torn knelt there, considering his options. He could wait for daylight or move in now. He could lurk in the grass and pick them off as they came out. Or he could bust in with guns blazing and no quarter given.

He decided not to wait. He still had a couple of hours of moonlight, and vision was good.

The door of the sod house faced south, with a window on either side. On the west side—the side nearest Torn—was another window. He moved to his left twenty paces and checked the north side, the one facing the river. No door or window. And the chimney stood on the east side.

One door and three windows, and all but one window on the same side of the house. Torn stared at the chimney. His smile was grim. Yes, that might work.

Returning to the claybank, he untied the blanket rolled up behind the cantle of his saddle. Mounting up, he draped the blanket across the pommel and put the claybank into a walk. He rode straight for the sod house, angling to arrive at the northwest corner. If someone happened to glance out that west window they would see him. But he rode on. The angle of his approach put the sod house between him and the rope corral. The horses there would not see him, nor would they pick up his scent, as long as the wind held from the south. The creak of saddle leather was not loud enough to betray him, and the claybank made no sound.

Closer now, he began to hear voices from inside. He paid them no attention, concentrating instead on the job at hand. Checking the claybank at the corner of the house, he dropped the reins to ground-hitch the horse and wrapped the blanket around his Winchester. Then he stood up on the saddle and hoisted himself onto the flat roof.

He had no doubt that the roof would hold him. It was made of thick sod supported on stout posts. He walked to the east end of the house, cat-footed, to the chimney. The voices were very clear now, and he sat on his heels to listen for a moment.

Treadway was talking. He sounded agitated.

"I thought you boys were professionals. I'm offering one or all of you good money to do what you do for a living."

"A thousand dollars to kill a federal judge?" Torn recognized this voice as well. It was Booth. "They'd put five thousand up for the price on my head if I killed a federal judge. And hell, I can barely walk or ride, as it is. You can see for yourself that me and Sam Cherokee here are kinda laid up. You should've done it, Treadway. Instead of running out here you should've walked up to that tall bastard and put a bullet in him your own self. Instead, you hightail it out here. We thought we were nice and safe here, but I ain't so sure now. What if Torn comes after you?"

"He doesn't know about this place," said Treadway.

"Now how come that don't ease my mind?" asked Booth dryly. "You say Farnum confessed to killing Lane Terrill."

"Yes, but Farnum didn't know about this place. Unless one of you told him. He never came out here."

"You sound scared, Mister Treadway." This was Grizzly, his voice deep and rumbling.

"And you're not thinking straight," added Booth.

"Don't forget who you work for," said Treadway, blustering.

"I think I just quit. Got any objections?"

A tense silence. Then Treadway spoke again. "What about you, Kid? I'll make it two thousand."

"Maybe. No offense, Mister Treadway," said The Cimarron Kid politely, "but do you have two thousand?"

"Right there in those saddlebags."

Another stretch of silence.

"Looks like more than two thousand," observed The Kid.

"I'll need a grubstake. I'll have to start all over somewhere else."

"How much is it, Kid?" asked Booth.

"Wait a minute . . ." began Treadway, edgy.

Booth chuckled. It wasn't a pretty sound. "We could just ventilate you, Treadway, and split that money among ourselves. What do you say, Sam? Grizzly?"

"I say no," said The Kid, as calmly as if he were discussing the weather.

Torn smiled grimly. The thieves were having a falling out.

"I've never turned on anyone I ever worked for," continued The Kid. "And I don't aim to start now."

"Thanks, Kid," breathed Treadway fervently.

"That's you, Kid," sneered Booth. "Not me."

"Well, I still work for Mister Treadway. And since this is Mister Treadway's money, I reckon I'll have to make sure he keeps it. So if you want to try and take it, Booth, go ahead and try."

Torn half expected gunplay to ensue. Instead, Booth muttered, "Hell. I don't care about the damned money that much, anyway. Go ahead and take Treadway's offer, Kid. You kill that judge and you'll be doing us all a favor."

"I guess I will," said The Kid.

The icy finger of dread traced Torn's spine.

In a fair fight he stood no chance against The Cimarron Kid, and he was wise enough to know it. It was not a good feeling, knowing that the fastest gun on the frontier had just hired out to kill you.

CHAPTER 23

TORN TOOK A DEEP, CALMING BREATH.

It was time to start the shindig.

He stood up and stuffed the blanket down into the chimney. The effect was not immediately noticed in the room below.

Treadway said, "How are you going to do it, Kid?"

"A fair fight. That's the only way I work. You know that, Mister Treadway. I'm not a back shooter."

"What are you lookin' at me for?" queried Booth. But there was no challenge in his voice. He had already decided it would be fatally unwise to provoke The Cimarron Kid.

"I'll call him out," said The Kid. "A man like Judge Torn won't back down."

"In front of God and everybody," said Treadway, and chuckled with delight. "You'll go down in history,

Kid. The judge is something of a legend. Like Earp and Hickok and Masterson. You'll make a name for yourself with this one. The man who gunned down Clay Torn."

"It will get me hanged," said The Kid flatly. "But then, I never wanted to live forever."

Torn shook his head. The Cimarron Kid was a strange one. Young, intelligent, well mannered—and a killer with a death wish. A boy with one unswerving desire: to die famous in a blaze of glory. Why? How had he come to this? Who was he, really? Where did he come from? What had turned him into The Cimarron Kid?

"Hey!" exclaimed Booth, coughing. "What the hell . . . ?"

"Where's that smoke coming from?" wondered Treadway, and started hacking, too.

There followed a chorus of coughing and curses. Torn walked to the south rim of the roof and stood directly above the door.

The first man out was one Torn did not recognize: a stocky, bandy-legged man with flat coarse features and shoulder-length black hair. Sam Cherokee, no doubt. The breed stumbled out of the smoke, wiping at his stinging eyes and bent over at the waist, gagging.

"Hey," said Torn.

Sam Cherokee whirled. He did not know where the voice had come from. Torn saw the six-shooter in the breed's hand and jacked a round into the breech of his Winchester.

"Drop the hog leg," he said, knowing all along it was advice Sam Cherokee would not heed.

The breed looked up and saw Torn.

"It's a trap!" he yelled to the others, still in the sod house. Then he swung his pistol up.

Torn fired from the hip, worked the action, fired again. Sam Cherokee performed a jerky dance as the slugs tore into him. He was dead before he hit the ground.

Booth and Grizzly bolted next. They headed straight for the rope corral, Grizzly in a lumbering run, Booth lurching on his injured leg. Both men fired up at the roof. Torn dropped Booth first. The gun slick fell, shot through the chest. He tried to sit up, tried to lift his Colt for one more shot. He was drooling blood. Torn took careful aim and fired. The bullet struck Booth in the center of the forehead and slammed him to the ground. His body spasmed, legs jerking wildly, and then was still.

Torn looked for Grizzly, but the big man had moved with surprising quickness and reached the rope corral. All Torn could see at first were the horses milling about. Then one broke away from the rest and vaulted the rope, and Torn realized Grizzly was bent low on the horse's back. Torn broke into a run, angling for the northeast corner of the roof. Grizzly was headed for the river. Would he pass close enough to the sod house? Reaching the corner, Torn had only a split second to make a decision.

Dropping the Winchester, he leaped.

He struck the horse on the haunches, hooked his left arm around Grizzly. The horse stumbled, then crow-hopped. Torn fell off, but he took Grizzly with him. They rolled down the slope. Torn lost his hold on the man, bounced to his feet. Growling like his namesake, Grizzly got up and pulled the trigger of his Walker Colt. The old thumb buster dry-fired. Cursing,

Grizzly hurled the pistol away and came at Torn, arms open wide, like he wanted a hug. It would be, Torn knew, a deadly embrace. He drew the Colt Peacemaker.

"Stay where you are," he snapped.

"Better shoot," roared Grizzly. "I'll snap your spine clean in half."

"Stand back," said Torn, and stepped away.

Grizzly laughed. "I'll tear your arms right off. I'll break your rib cage open and rip out your heart. What's the matter, Judge? Why don't you shoot?"

"I've never shot an unarmed man."

"Then die," leered Grizzly, and lunged, his monstrous hands groping for Torn.

Torn fanned the hammer of the Colt Peacemaker. He fired all six rounds into Grizzly. The first two stopped the goliath, the next two sent him staggering backward, and the last two put him down.

"There's a first time for everything," muttered Torn.

When he heard the gunshot he was already falling, the impact, like being hit in the side with an ax handle, knocking him off his feet. He rolled a little way down the slope and lay sprawled on his back, gasping. He'd been shot enough times to know it had happened again.

He put his right hand on his left side, below the rib cage, probing gingerly. It came away sticky with warm blood. That was good. The bullet had gone through him in a place where there were no vital organs.

"I got him!" yelled Treadway, exultant. "I got the bastard, Kid! Hey? Kid?"

Cursing himself for being a careless fool, Torn realized he had left the Winchester on the roof of the sod house and that the Colt in his hand was empty. That figured. He was in a bad spot now. He watched Treadway coming down the slope and lay perfectly still, his eyes almost closed.

"I got you, you sonuvabitch," said Treadway, looming over him.

He pointed his rifle at Torn's head.

Torn struck quick as lightning. He grabbed the barrel of the rifle, turning it aside and pulling at the same time. The rifle went off. The muzzle-flash momentarily blinded him. The bullet drilled the ground inches from his head. Treadway tried to hold onto the rifle and pulled off balance. He tripped over Torn and went sprawling. Torn rolled on top of him. He tried to bring the barrel of the Colt down on Treadway's skull, but the blow was poorly aimed and struck Treadway in the shoulder instead. Treadway roared and connected with a backhand blow that knocked Torn ten feet. Stunned, Torn scrambled up. Treadway was already standing. He yanked a pistol out of his belt. Torn hurled the empty Colt at him. That bought him a couple of seconds. Precious time. The difference between life and death. Because while Treadway ducked, Torn drew the saber knife from its shoulder rig. All he had to do was thumb the rawhide loop off the pommel and the knife slipped into his waiting hand. As Treadway raised his pistol, Torn threw the saber knife. It wasn't balanced for throwing, but he had learned to hurl it effectively at close range in an underhand throw.

Treadway stared in disbelief at the knife buried to the hilt in his belly. He forgot all about shooting.

Closing fast, Torn wrenched the pistol out of Treadway's grasp. Treadway's startled eyes rose slowly to meet Torn's flinty gaze.

"Help . . . help me . . ."

Torn thought about Lane Terrill and Matt Caldwell and Sheriff Mackey and Lotus, and even the cowboy Treadway had beaten to death with his fists years ago.

No mercy.

He grabbed the knife and turned it just so. The blade ripped up into Treadway's heart.

Treadway died instantly.

Torn felt the earth tremble beneath his feet, heard the sound of horses on the run.

A moment later, a dozen riders appeared on the crest of the ridge, swarming around the sod house.

Torn retrieved the knife and trudged wearily up the slope. Andy Terrill rode down to meet him.

"Judge, are you . . . My God, you've been shot. Jericho!"

The black cowboy spurred his horse down toward them.

"No," said Torn. "I'm all right."

But he felt strange. Light-headed. He looked up at the sky. The stars were spinning.

"I'm all right," he mumbled, and fell.

Jericho executed a running dismount and caught him, laid him gently down.

When he came to it was daylight. He was sitting up against the back of the sod house. He had a nice view of the Niobrara. The surface of the river looked like molten gold in the morning light. A haze clung to the low places in the hills that seemed to roll on and on in all directions. A thin swirl of mare's tail clouds looked like wagon tracks in sand on the pale blue sky, and the sun, just now rising, touched them with dabs of pink and gold.

Close by, the T Bar range riders were hunkered down around a cookfire. Seeing Torn awake, Andy walked over.

"How do you feel?"

"Like I've been shot."

"The bullet went through."

Torn nodded. He felt the tight dressing around his midsection.

"Jericho's handiwork," said Andy. "He cauterized the bullet holes with gunpowder set afire."

"Sorry I missed that."

Jericho arrived with a cup of steaming coffee, offered it to Torn. Torn took it, sipped gratefully, and decided he was going to live after all.

"What are you all doing here?" he asked.

"Rose Pendergast sent a rider out to the ranch," said Andy. "Told us where you were heading and what you were up against. We thought we better come along."

"You should have seen Dusty's face when he knew he was going to miss a fight on account of that busted leg," said Jericho. "He'll feel some better when he finds out we missed it, too."

"We buried the dead," said Andy.

"How many did you bury?" asked Torn, his voice hollow.

"Four. Why?"

"The Kid got away, then."

"Who?"

"The Cimarron Kid."

Jericho threw an apprehensive look around.

"He's long gone by now," said Torn. "I reckon I'll see him again, though."

He stood up, leaning against the wall of the sod house for support.

"You should take it slow, Judge," admonished Andy.

"I can ride. Where's my horse?"

"I'll fetch him," said Jericho.

"I'll go back to town with you," offered Andy. "Just to make sure you get there."

Torn looked off at the horizon with narrowed eyes.

"I'm not going back to Valentine."

"Why not?"

"My work is done here."

"Yes, but . . . well, it's certainly none of my business, but there seems to be a woman there who cares a great deal about you."

"That's why I'm not going back."

"I don't understand."

Torn smiled bleakly. "Not sure I do, either."

Jericho returned with the claybank, saddled and ready. Torn noticed the Winchester in its scabbard. His gun belt and shoulder rig were draped over the saddle horn. His shirt and frock coat were lying across the cantle. The shirt was covered with bloodstains. Torn tossed it away and put the frock coat on, with Andy's help. Wincing at the pain, he climbed into the saddle, took the reins from Jericho.

"Thanks for all you've done, Judge," said Andy.

"You'll do fine out here, Andy."

"No doubt about that," agreed Jericho. "He's every bit the man his father was, ask me."

"Want me to tell her anything?" Andy asked Torn.

"Tell her . . ." Torn shook his head. "No. I'll tell her myself, when I see her again. So long."

He turned the lanky claybank east, into the rising sun, following that lonesome trail he knew so well.

Saddle-up to these

THE REGULATOR by Dale Colter
Sam Slater, blood brother of the Apache and a cunning bounty-hunter, is out to collect the big price on the heads of the murderous Pauley gang. He'll give them a single choice: surrender and live, or go for your sixgun.

THE REGULATOR—Diablo At Daybreak
by Dale Colter
The Governor wants the blood of the Apache murderers who ravaged his daughter. He gives Sam Slater a choice: work for him, or face a noose. Now Slater must hunt down the deadly renegade Chacon…Slater's Apache brother.

THE JUDGE by Hank Edwards
Federal Judge Clay Torn is more than a judge—sometimes he has to be the jury and the executioner. Torn pits himself against the most violent and ruthless man in Kansas, a battle whose final verdict will judge one man right…and one man dead.

THE JUDGE—War Clouds
by Hank Edwards
Judge Clay Torn rides into Dakota where the Cheyenne are painting for war and the army is shining steel and loading lead. If war breaks out, someone is going to make a pile of money on a river of blood.